W9-BLB-583

MUCH YOUNGER MAN

Published by
Soho Press Inc.
853 Broadway
New York, NY 10003

Library of Congress Cataloging-in-Publication Data

Highbridge, Dianne
A much younger man / Dianne Highbridge.
p.   cm.
ISBN 1-56947-147-9 (alk. paper)
I. Title.
PR9619.3.H5332M83   1998
823--dc21

97-43708
CIP

10 9 8 7 6 5 4 3 2 1

A

MUCH YOUNGER MAN

DIANNE HIGHBRIDGE

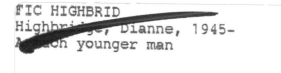
SOHO

FOR M.L.G.
WITH LOVE

A
MUCH YOUNGER MAN

CHAPTER ONE

A boy on the train, that's all. Shirt flopping out at the back, fair hair falling into his eyes, a bag of books hefted over his shoulder. Coming from school.

As she is, too, with a briefcase full of work, of papers inept or effusive or snappily confident, all to be read, corrected, marked in her impatient hand, at the kitchen table late on Sunday night, with the help of a glass of white wine—safer than red, should she from clumsiness or frustration knock it over. It happens.

This boy shouts goodbye to a couple of mates getting off at a station where jacarandas drip their petals over the fence, the platform carpeted with purple in the afternoon light. That's what makes her notice him, the shout. Then he turns and comes towards her, down the half-empty, swaying carriage.

He seems to be looking directly at her. He is. Oh, no. He sits down beside her. A juvenile nut? The hardest to get rid of, and the last thing she needs.

"Aly?"

Not a nut, and not just a boy on a train. A boy who knows her name. An inward sigh. Whose boy is this? A neighbour's, glimpsed on a Saturday morning in the driveway, sloshing water over the family car? A colleague's, met briefly in the smoky dusk of some backyard party? Whose? They grow so bloody fast, and they mostly look roughly like this. Tallish for their ages, taller than kids used to be for their ages, that is. More or less golden, relatively unafflicted by acne or irregular teeth, with eyes whose colour she never really notices, brown or blue or hazel. This one's eyes are not exactly blue. He could be any one of half a dozen silky-haired sons. He does look familiar, come to think of it. Be non-committal. "Hi," she says.

"Haven't seen you for a while."

"No, right." Whose?

"Still teaching? Same school?"

"Mm."

"Don't know how you do it."

"Me either."

"I'd hate to teach people like me."

Rude, since this is a pleasantry, to say I do hate it. And not always true. "So you don't want to be a teacher."

Of course not. These kids all want to be record producers or something. Anything, as long as it's not in a field where they might actually expect to get a job. And their parents can afford their fantasies. That's what being middle class means.

He looks surprised. "I haven't changed my mind. Remember the verandah city? Zelda fell into it. She got dizzy, spinning." He laughs. "Disaster!"

Problem solved. Louise's Tom. Good God. His legs sprawl into the aisle. That's a lot of height in— however long it's been. She's seen Louise on occasion in spite of the coolness, heard the updates on him, his talent and creativity, blah blah, to which she's never listened very closely, but he was nowhere near this tall last time she actually saw him. Appearing on command with Zelda, his little sister, to say hello. Darting away.

"I remember the city."

"You should, you built a tower."

"You remember that!"

"I do. The only thing left standing. It was structurally sound, see?"

"But you were only— How old are you now?"

"Fifteen. You didn't know me, did you?"

"Of course I knew you."

He chuckles. No longer a little boy's voice. "It's OK. I don't blame you." He turns in the seat, to face her. "I saw you from down there, but I wasn't sure at first, either. You've done something to your hair. It's redder. It used to be sort of mousy."

Thanks, kid. Now it's sort of grey. "I put henna in it."

He considers. "Good idea."

"Well. So . . . you still draw buildings?"

"I'm better at it now."

"Still play the guitar?"

"Yeah, and the lute."

"The what?" The train screeches to a halt between stations. Ferns cling to the seeping black sandstone walls of the cutting. Green light filters into the carriage. How long are we going to be sitting here?

"The lute." Good, we've started again. "Louise wanted me to do it." Naturally. Very Louise. "You know. Got to be different. But I've got a great teacher, and I'm getting into it. Weird, isn't it? Must be in the genes, the early stuff."

"Don't you get a bit of flak about it at school?"

"Not much. It's not as if I don't like anything else. And there's a kid in my class who does ballet. He catches most of it."

"Lucky for you."

"He's not gay. You know, that's what the flak's about. He gets the last laugh."

"Well, then." Almost her stop. It's been a hard week. "And you swim?" He did, didn't he? He had asthma, and Louise—

"We do pretty well in the medley relay."

"School team?"

"Backstroke. My best stroke." He stretches unself-consciously, hands linked behind his head. "I haven't got asthma any more. I grew out of it."

"Good." There's a silence. "Good," she says again. What else? "I like backstroke. I like looking up at the sky."

"That's what I like."

She gathers up her things. "The next stop's mine."

"Are you going home?"

"I'm going to my yoga class."

"What kind?"

"What do you mean what kind?"

"Aren't there different kinds?"

"Hatha. Plain old hatha yoga."

He stands to let her pass. "You're not allowed to say how tall I've grown. Seems to be taboo."

She has to look up at him. "You might get embarrassed."

"I don't," he says cheerfully. "What are you smiling at?"

"Just remembered, she wanted to call you Piers."

"Was it you that talked her out of it? Not easy, I owe you one. You should have been there for Griselda, she's stuck with it."

"I was living in London then." No, I was living in hell. And Louise kept writing to me. With her work and the kids she had time to write the letters I needed, to help me live through it. "Give my love to your— to Louise and Toby."

"I will. Come round some time."

"Thanks." She makes her way down the aisle. The train jolts coming into the station, and she has to grab at a handle in an undignified manner. But when she looks back he isn't smirking, he's just smiling. Then his face changes, and he leaps up with her briefcase in his hand, and hurtles down after her. The essays!

"Thanks," she says again, and this time it's heartfelt. "Thank you, Tom."

"Be careful, there's a gap."

He remains standing by the door as it closes, arms folded. He has a swimmer's long torso. Awkward when his legs are in the way, but graceful like that. From the platform, she sees his hand raised in casual salute, and, just as casually, returns it.

The archer. Helps concentration, and reduces the hips. Breathe in. Left foot across right thigh. Grasp with right hand, touch right toes with left hand. Louise's Tom. How about that? Nice kid. The day Toby rang. He's born! Toby always said it would be a boy, and Toby generally gets what he wants. None of our friends had babies yet, this was the first. Louise would have to be first. I went out and bought a . . . what? A bunny-rug, yellow, so as not to be sexist. A present. I took it to the hospital, and the baby was in Louise's room. She'd had everything natural, and she was going to carry him on her back in a thing, a kind of sling, from some tribe in the Amazon. She did, too. That anthropologist friend whose name I forget had brought it. They bond better in the Amazon because of this, she said. So young, we were. Now we're . . . where's the time gone? Where's it going? Exhale. Left foot to right ear. I'm thirty-five, it's incredible. Some days I believe it, not every day. Oh, my God. Just now I do. It has been a hard week. This is hard. Breathe in. Return. Repeat on other side. How much longer can I stand this job? I've been doing it most of his life. Only that time out in the middle, when I went so far from home with Eric. Exhale. That was a mistake. Right foot to left ear. I wish I could remember why . . . why did I do that? Why did I even think of it, when it was bound to be . . . bound to be . . . Hold it there.

Concentrate, says the teacher. I am concentrating. This is what it's for. A sunny child. That time when he was two or so, he fell and cut his head, blood everywhere. He had stitches, and he didn't cry, and minutes later he was laughing. Louise cried for him. She said, he's so happy, sometimes I wonder if he's all there. He is all there. Oh, yes. Breathe in. Return.

The weekend. Lots to do. That rootbound philodendron, and the dwarf lemon. Out of potting mix, buy more. Repotting is always satisfying. Tap the pot, remove the plant, reduce the size of the root ball by gently pulling away the old soil, trim the roots. Repot with fresh mixture. Water, not too wet. Sit back on heels, look at pot for a while.

Saturday night, dinner and a movie with Katie, who leers at the waiter when he brings her goat cheese pizza. "I can't help it," she says, "Brian's away. I think my hormones get all screwed up when I'm alone. Oh, I'm sorry, Aly! I didn't mean that!"

Pages of familiar handwriting move from the right side of the table, stare up briefly, and, scratched in red, vanquished, retreat to the left. The two piles are about the same height. Half-done. A sip.

Damian. Marilee. Tiffany. Knowing little thing, that one. Probably knows more than I do about practically everything. But not too much about the dramatic function of the witches in *Macbeth*. She'll survive.

The phone. She reaches out her left hand for it, scribbles a mark with her right, adds Tiffany to the left pile, thus tipping the balance, draws Kim from the middle of the right pile. It's important to maintain an element of surprise. Or pathetic, depending how you look at it.

"Alyson, Louise McCarthy."

"Louise." Not really unexpected, this. Why does she always

say her full name? How many Louises does she think I know?

"We were just thinking about you. Tom says he met you on Friday."

"I hardly recognised him."

"Isn't he something?"

"Yes."

"Did he tell you about the recital?"

"No. No, he didn't."

"This early music group. He filled in for them, they needed a lute at short notice. The consort, it's a viol, and a chitarrone, two lutes, but the other one's his teacher, all professionals—"

A sound in the background, barely audible, but the intonation is unmistakably that of "Mum, shut up!"

"He doesn't like me talking about it," says Louise. "He's very—"

"Modest." Eyes raised ceilingwards.

"He doesn't realise, he's so—" In the background, a groan. "Anyway. We were thinking, if you're not too pressed in the middle of the week, would you like to come and have dinner with us on Wednesday?"

"Um . . ." Who else? Oliver the architect, whose type I'm not? The wine-freaks, the ones with the share in the vineyard? Worse, some wimp meant just for me, some visiting lecturer with a great line in Post-Structuralist Theory? To make sure Toby doesn't do it again?

"Only us, nothing fancy. Pasta, glass of red. It's been ages."

It has indeed been ages since the night Toby nuzzled her neck in the kitchen after a party, among all the scraps and empties, and she told him where to go. Toby, fearing she'd rat on him, apparently told his own version, preemptively, so to speak. Hence the coolness. Louise is a smart woman, but not that smart. Who is? On the other hand, she hasn't broken off relations entirely, there's been lunch now and then with Katie, so there must be a window of doubt. Is Louise getting jumpy, is Toby losing his nerve, after all these years?

Not as if she's been the only one. Far from it, that's well known. Or as if it were the first time, which, if she remembers right, was in their first little terrace house, also in the kitchen, while Louise was nursing Tom in the living room. She'd offered to do the washing up because it's such a drag watching someone breastfeed, especially Louise, so very conscious of the maternal picture, carrying on a conversation with the grunting baby that admitted of no third or fourth parties, requiring only silent admiration, the most difficult kind. Toby came out and said, God, I'm so bored, and ran a fingertip around the neck of her blouse, and she giggled, and it was actually almost a temptation.

That was just before the open-marriage period. A curious interlude. Jealousy is the least productive of emotions, the least creative, proclaimed Louise in the throes of this particular idea.

If someone wants to dance, or eat a meal, with the person you're married to, that's all right, isn't it? Why should fucking be any different? For a moment there, Louise actually seemed to be offering her Toby, but only in principle.

Poor old Toby. Not that it matters. They're still together, and not in that pokey little place either, but in a vast house renovated by Oliver, Tom's godfather, the perpetrator of edifices all over the city with facades that look like the backs of refrigerators, but even he couldn't do much to hurt the old sandstone house by the harbour.

And there they live among the trees and the birds, with a delicious breeze off the water on the hottest day, Toby, Louise, Tom, Griselda, and their old, environmentally incorrect cat ("She won't be replaced"), Satori. Louise hasn't done too badly, has she?

She drives to school this morning. The *Concierto de Aranjuez* on the cassette player, to soothe. Pulls into the gate just behind Mel. Out of the corner of her eye she can see the Boss already standing in front of his office with his prized antique pocket watch held ostentatiously in his hand, but there's plenty of time. He likes to intimidate, to see you hustle.

She wrestles her bag out of the car, leans against the door, fumbles her key into the lock.

There's a bunch of Year Eights scuffling on the other side of the parking-lot fence. Some kick-boxing going on. Not apparently with much ill-will, but nevertheless strictly verboten. The force they put behind each blow, the incredible energy they have in everything! It makes her feel tired, and Monday morning hasn't even begun.

"You boys!" bellows Mel, and they are instantly subdued, and melt away.

"How do you do that?"

"Force of intellect." She grins. "You don't want a kitten, do you?"

"No, thanks."

"Sure? Our cat had five last night, all over my hockey kit. They're going to be lovely."

"Alice?"

"Gertrude. Little slut."

"Who's a little slut?" He does this, Bill, comes up behind you, grabs at the tail of your conversation. The words are a gift.

"Never mind, Bill. No-one who'd be interested in you."

Alyson moves away. Don't give him any chances. One Friday night at the pub, which she doesn't do any more, he whispered in her ear: "Can I whisper sweet nothings?" And she said, "I didn't think you knew any, Bill. I've heard the way you talk to your wife." That one rejection, ill considered, was enough. He'll now go very far out of his way to make her look a fool. At staff meetings, everything she says, he makes it sound like the stupidest thing he's ever heard. Easily done if you want to, and he does.

Slip up the stairs, dump books and papers, cross the yard to Assembly, stand quietly at the back. Ignore all violations, short of actual bodily harm. There's Tiffany and her gang with skirts taken up even higher over the weekend. Devoted little seamstresses they are. Funny, when I started I used to want to do away with the whole uniform code. In the interests of personal freedom. I really thought reason would prevail. This wasn't what I meant, Tiffany's bum. What's the delay? Just get on with it. Oh, I forgot, the mayor's here, to talk about . . . What's the pretext? You are the leaders of tomorrow —too much! The old Leaders of Tomorrow speech. How do they do it, straight-faced? A titter. He's forgotten the Boss's name. Things are looking up.

Warm morning, open window. The smell of adolescents en masse, stronger as the day wears on. As individuals, they're maniacally showered and shampooed, but there it is, pungent. There may be charm in the gawky doe-like stage, but I can't see it at this moment. A couple of unfortunate pimple-pickers in this lot, too. Distract them. True, though I'm not up to Mel's standards as a disciplinarian, I don't have the problems I used to have. That nightmare, I'd walk into the room and the big boys would be tossing something around from desk to desk at the back, and I'd walk up there and hold out my hand for whatever it was (worse if I saw it in my dream, a tiny dead animal, something slimy). Instead of giving it to me they'd throw it on the floor, and then I'd say, pick it up, another mistake, pitting my will directly against theirs, and they'd have my measure, and they'd refuse, and I'd wake up sweating. Nothing like that happens now, in the class or in my dreams. I don't know when it stopped, when I learned. I got better. I adjusted.

Kylie, read. "Out, damned spot!" Is that so funny? Ah. Your dog's called Spot. Look, you can read it funny or you can read it straight. You think they give Oscars for giggling? Best Giggler in a Tragedy? Come on.

The first day I taught, as a proper qualified teacher, I walked between the rows of desks in the first classroom that was really mine, feeling unbelievably adult. I had them writing. I thought, this is easy, after all. They were quiet, it was all quiet, there was a lawn mower outside, at a distance, only that peaceful sound. And then I thought: is this what I'm doing for the rest of my life? That moment, when the room full of kids closed up around me! When I realised what a mistake I'd made, from which so many other mistakes arose. Even the mistake of marrying, of leaping at the chance to leave. But I came home, and I was lucky to get back into the job at all. It gives a different perspective. Even though kids are tougher now; they'll say, "fuck you." I don't care. I don't care enough. I don't need them to love me. I just do it. I can. Year after year, they go by. They're always the same, only I get older. I see them sometimes, in the supermarket, in the dry cleaner's, at the ballet. They've graduated, they're married. Sometimes there's a baby, and it grasps my finger, and I praise it. She's going to be a better student than me, they always say. Sometimes a sad story as we stand there in the mall by racks of T-shirts, the smell of doughnuts in the air. They remember my name, I pretend I remember theirs, that they're more than faces to me. It usually works. And I don't need promotion. I'd hate to be standing right now in front of one of those immense schedules covered in all different colours: times, people, rooms. The computer humming. If I'm going to do it, I suppose I'll take the kids.

Come what come may, Time and the hour runs through the roughest day. Macbeth.

Tiffany, falling into step with her between classes, asks, "What d'you think about IVF?" Tiffany's mother, it appears, had lots of it and was mad as a cut snake when it didn't work the first seven times, happy as anything when it did, and produced—"Da-daa! Me!"

"So it was all worth it."

"Are you kidding? It was worth it. To them. To me too. You know, I'm here. Talking to you."

"I'm kidding."

"But d'you mind paying taxes for it?"

"Ask me again after I've seen your test."

Sitting at the table in the staff room eating a carton of apricot yoghurt, she thinks of old teachers she used to know. Fingers stained with nicotine and dusty with chalk. Sticklers. What they said at Teachers' College, that last lecture, not entirely tongue in cheek. Rule One: never use someone else's cup. Forget Philosophy of Education. Have your own mug.

She has.

What music would he play on the lute?

CHAPTER TWO

$\mathcal{L}$ouise is slicing vegetables. She knows the right way to chop and slice every different kind of thing, and holds the knife just so, as in those diagrams you see in the front of cookbooks. Once, at Alyson's own place, Louise snatched the knife out of her hand and showed her how to slice carrots properly. Louise always knew that you never put pineapple in a curry. She served gazpacho before anyone else had heard of it, discovered extra-virgin cold-pressed olive oil, made both yeast and sourdough bread, steeped herbs in vinegar, and for a whole decade despised meringue in all its forms. But there, thinks Alyson, she was wrong.

"You're not on a diet, are you? I've got a real dessert for you. Mascarpone, amaretti, brandy, cream. The works, Alyson!"

Should I be on a diet? "Sounds like I will be tomorrow."

"That's a lovely top you're wearing," says Louise, bringing the flat of her knife down hard on a giant clove of garlic. "Those pretty squiggly things, and the subtle colours. Is it batik?" She always comments on clothes, although she still mostly wears the trousers and shirts that suited her thinness when she was a student, and still suit her. Now the shirt will be silk, and she'll add a severely tailored black jacket. When they used to go shopping together, long ago, it was Alyson she encouraged to buy little print dresses with frills, and schoolmarmish wire-framed glasses, the kind of things, thinks Alyson, that if I wore them now I'd look . . . schoolmarmish. Then they were cute. But Louise was never cute. She always looked just as she does now. Cool, calm, pressed. Utterly different from me. The hair, too. Hers falls fine and straight to an unchanging point between chin and shoulder. She never permed it, she never wore plastic earrings.

How is it that two such different women have been friends for so long? Perhaps it's the difference that makes it possible, after all. I'm not a rival, in any sense. Even Toby—she can't help being careful, she can't afford to let down her guard there, but she must have had to use other weapons than mere coolness often enough, against women who'd be willing and well placed to take him up on it in a serious way. Young barristers, sexy in robes and wigs, all wit and hunger. It must be a torment. She can be indiscreet with me, too, and it won't put me in a position to hurt her career or anything. She can help me if I need it, knowing nothing I can do for her can ever compare, needing no return, keeping no balance sheet. The same is true of all the dinners I've had in her house. The pattern was set long ago, and neither of us is likely to break it now.

"Is it batik?" Louise repeats, scraping the garlic into the pan.

"Oh, sorry, that smells great. No, I don't think it is really. I just picked it up. I'm tempted to wear it every day to school, it's easy, I throw it on over something."

"How's school?"

"No less horrible than usual. How's . . . your work?" You can't say, how's university, it never sounds right.

"Oh, I've been having quite a time. You know Martin Japp, no, you've forgotten, you met him here once, a wimpy— Well, anyway, he got married. We've been editing this series together, and I tell you, the man is not pulling his weight. Who do you think's doing all the grunt-work? All the proofs? He keeps telling me about his domestic responsibilities. How busy his wife is, she's some sort of dentist, a periodontist, I don't know, why should I care? How he's got to get a child to kindergarten every morning, how he needs more time for his family. Imagine if I'd—when I'd just had Tom, and Toby was up all night preparing briefs, and I was finishing my Chaucer-meets-Boccaccio book, remember that, and being on not one but half a dozen committees—if I'd made *any* murmur, you know what they would have said, and now this little fuckwit—" She lowers her voice. "There's Tom, he's been at his lesson. You didn't say anything when you met him about how he's shot up, did you? Don't. They hate it."

Alyson takes an olive from the bowl Louise has put before her on the counter. Louise always has these wonderful, fat olives from the Greek delicatessen, scooped oozing oil and brine straight from one particular barrel. From the corner of her eye, through an archway, she sees him rest an odd-shaped case against a chair. She palms the seed.

"Did you see Griselda coming from the bus stop?" calls Louise.

"No," he says.

"She's late."

"She's always this late. So she's not really late."

Louise frowns, clicks her tongue, turns back to her sauce.

"Hello, Aly."

"She *is* late," mutters Louise.

"Karate," he explains. "Not splitting concrete blocks yet, but she's working on it." To Louise, he says, "I'll go and meet her if you like."

They hear the front door slam. "There you are, no need to start calling the police and all the hospitals after all," he says. "She has, you know."

"I know."

Griselda is a smaller, more solid and athletic young Louise. Her hair is cut very short, she wears several earrings and black high-top sneakers. In the archway, she whirls round to hug Toby, down from his study.

"I don't like her coming home so late, Toby," says Louise.

"No-one's going to mess with me, Mum. It's the way I walk. They can tell."

"It's just that attitude that worries me," snaps Louise. Then, "Darling, Alyson's here."

"So I see."

She half-rises from her stool to receive Toby's kiss. "Pink and pretty as ever," he murmurs, so only she can hear. He's as skilled at this seductive murmur as he must be at the courtroom purr or thunder, the robing room guffaw.

Louise, both hands occupied, offers him her cheek. "What do you think of the hair?"

"It's gorgeous." Thick and wavy, curling over his collar, it's suddenly gone all silver-grey.

"Don't you think he looks like Richard Gere?"

"Absolutely." As if the coolness had never been.

"Richard Gere's *old*," says Griselda.

Tom takes an olive, finds a saucer for the seeds, pushes it towards her. She lets the seed drop stickily from her hand, rubs her palms together. He pours himself a glass of wine.

"Only one for you before dinner," says Louise, not looking round.

Once, standing in front of the window of their old house, hands stuck in her pockets, watching the children playing outside in the sandpit Toby built for them, Louise suddenly said, "I want them to think well of themselves. Naturally. Not have to work at it, like me." The memory of this still surprises. Then, she was already an Associate Professor, about to become the youngest woman full Professor in the Department. Nothing has ever seemed to stand in her way, least of all doubt. Yet she works so hard at everything she touches, perhaps she did feel the need to work hard at herself too. Anyhow, the kids do think well of themselves. At dinner, Griselda sometimes verges on the obnoxious, but if Tom ever went through that stage, it must have been during the coolness. Now he just knows his own mind.

"Have you been to Italy, Aly?"

"A long time ago."

"Tom's in love with Italy," says Toby. "We were there last holidays. Rented a van. We did what we've wanted to do for years, we went to the ancestral village, where my grandfather came from."

"Where's that?"

"Tiny place in the Abruzzi. We met some cousins who lived in Melbourne years ago."

Griselda chimes in, "They had Australian accents, and they used slang we didn't even know!"

"Time warp." Toby tilts the bottle. "More wine, Aly?"

"There's a ruined castle," says Tom.

"If he discovers a ruin in the guidebook, there goes the schedule. He's got to climb all over it before you go any further."

"It's interesting, the foundations, and just the bare walls. You can see how they thought about building."

"He still wants to be an architect."

"Unless he does music," puts in Louise.

"I'm not going to do music."

"As if there aren't enough unemployed architects!"

"There are plenty of unemployed musicians," he points out. "Look. I'm not bad, I love it, but I'll never be as good as you think I am. And don't say I can be a scholar, or teach. I don't want to do anything like that. I'm practical."

This must be a variation on a dialogue they've had before. He's explaining his position, and it sounds as if he's prepared to do it as often as necessary. She envies him. It seems to her now that when she was his age, she knew next to nothing of what she wanted.

"All right, mate," says Toby. "All right, Louise. Let's not get into it now." He leans over, bottle in hand. "Alyson, you ever hear from Eric?"

"Eric? Why should I?"

"Saw him the other day, crossing Phillip Street. Tells me he's remarried, got a baby on the way. Still in her twenties. Works for Max, you remember Max, conveyancing."

"Lucky him. Lucky her."

"He looks well on it," says Toby, not innocently.

Louise's eyes meet Alyson's for a fraction of a second. "Then there's no justice," says Louise. "If there were, he'd be frying in hell with devils sticking pitchforks up his arse."

She's one of the few people who knows, thinks Alyson. She saw my bruises when I was still denying it, and she wasn't fooled. She was angry then, and she's angry even now, when I've grown so weary of anger.

Emotion stings behind her eyes. Toby too is silent, though whether he's been shamed, who can tell?

Griselda jumps up. "I've got to do my essay!"

"Bring it down and I'll go over it for you."

"Hands off, Mum," says Tom, quietly. "Let her do it."

Louise gives him an unreadable look.

"I can do it. Just takes a bit longer, that's all." They hear her pounding up the stairs.

"She's never been able to just *walk* anywhere." Louise is giving in! "Make the coffee, Toby. I've been meaning to ask Alyson about my pelargonium."

A ritual. Louise reads several languages and can hum her way through whole operas, but whatever the opposite of a green thumb is, she's got it. One of the smartest things about her, though, is that she never fails to allow other people their areas of expertise, and to give full credit, knowing it makes them happy.

Alyson follows her out onto the broad verandah. Through the trees, you can see the lights of the harbour. There's that expensive cool breeze.

Louise, leaning against the railing, pulls a pack of cigarettes from her shirt pocket, and a lighter. "They won't let me smoke inside any more," she says. "The cigarette police, in my own home. You see how I'm treated? They can be so bloody self-righteous, kids."

Alyson crouches by the pot, gently lifts a leaf with her forefinger.

"They're characters."

"I wanted them to be. But Tom—he's so changed. He doesn't come anywhere with us any more, not since Italy. He's not rebellious, exactly, it's just that he's got an inner life we know nothing about. He goes our way only if it happens to coincide with his own. Otherwise, forget it."

The leaf is yellow in the light that streams out from the living room. "Wasn't he always like that?" Wasn't there always a reserve, along with the sweetness, and a touch of her own steel?

"Now, more than ever!" The breeze catches at Louise's cigarette, makes it glow. "And he's so tall. You have to come to terms
with your own—" She pauses, then shrugs. "Your own age. I
mean, another few years and he could be making me a grandmother."

"Or less."

"Don't even think it. You can talk to them about condoms till
the cows come home!"

"I think you're overfeeding."

"How do you know?"

"Look how your leaves are dropping."

"I gave them some of those vitamin capsules."

"These don't need much. Don't water them too often, either.
They like it dry."

"I'll remember." Louise taps her ash into a tub of fern. "Alyson,
take no notice of Toby. About Eric."

"It's all right."

"Just be glad you never got pregnant. You'd never have been
rid of him."

No, there'd be no peace for me, even now. "At least I had that
much sense."

"You did. You had enough."

Tom appears, silhouetted against the doorway. In his hand, he
holds a slice of bread and jam. "There she is," he says.

High up in the gum tree nearest the house is a possum. Seeing the bread, she climbs cautiously down the trunk to a lower branch. She scans the garden, then hops lightly onto the railing.

"You shouldn't make her dependent on you, Tom," says Louise.

"That's why I don't do it every night. It's just a treat." He holds out the bread to the possum, who takes it in both paws. While they watch, she begins to nibble at the crust, her large eyes moving from face to face, pink nose quivering. "She likes the strawberry better than the plum."

"Are you sure it's a she?" asks Alyson.

"She used to come down with a baby on her back. And I know it's her. See the ragged ear? She must know how to take care of herself."

"I wish I thought you did," says Louise, reaching up slowly, so as not to startle, stroking the hair back from his forehead. He's not one of those soft-faced, full-lipped boys. There's a symmetry of brow and nose and jaw. Fine-textured skin. Nothing extra. He inclines his head slightly, not embarrassed but not paying much attention either, his eyes on the animal.

The possum has finished the bread, and is delicately licking the jam from each paw, when next door a dog barks. Instantly, she leaps. Almost flying, she disappears into the bush. A split second later they hear the crash in the underbrush where she lands.

"Let's go in," says Louise. "Tom can play us something. He *is* good, you know."

He doesn't say anything, but by the time the women, talking, come back into the bright room, he's disappeared, and so has his lute.

He's on the train again. He acknowledges her with a nod, and when his friends get off, he joins her as if it's a matter of course. "I waited for you," he says. "Now I know you get this train on Fridays."

She marks her place in the book she's reading. "Sometimes I drive. It depends how I feel, what I've got to do."

"That's OK. But if you're on this one, we can talk." He takes the book from her hands, to see the title. Blood drips from the dagger on the cover.

"It's not as bad as it looks," she says defensively. Which is ridiculous.

"You can always say it's subversive, or transgressive."

"Picked up a few things, haven't you?"

"Here and there." He returns the book. His shirtsleeves are rolled up to the elbow, his forearms smooth, with fine dark gold hair. Pretty, she thinks. "Did you wonder why I didn't play the other night?"

"No. I just assumed you didn't feel like it."

"I didn't. Not like that, on show." Then he says, with the barest pause: "I would've played for you."

A small alarm bell rings somewhere in her head. She looks quickly at him, half-afraid to see the tell-tale intensity of an incipient crush in his eyes. Not really a problem if so, but better if not. He's looking straight back at her. His eyes aren't almost blue, as she thought, they're grey, and completely guileless. Somehow this is not reassuring. "I'd like to hear you some day, but I don't know much about that kind of music," she says.

"You don't have to. You'll see."

All she has to do next Friday is drive. Or get a different train. Earlier, later. Either way. She does none of these things. She gets the same train, and sits in the same carriage.

He tells her about famous architects. Brunelleschi, Bernini, these she's heard of. Then there are more recent ones, Mario Botta, Carlo Scarpa. All Italian. "I like some of the Japanese too," he says. "Do you know Isozaki?"

She shakes her head. She thinks of architects, if at all, as being mostly like his godfather, an egomaniac who talks a great building, but that's about it. "Would you like to work with Oliver?"

"Not really," he says. "Oliver's a pure modernist."

This doesn't sound like a very good thing to be. "I love the

Opera House," she ventures. "I mean, like everyone else. It'd be more original to hate it."

"Who cares? It's a building you can love! I've loved it since I was a kid. We used to sail over there, you know Dad had that old eighteen-footer? Sailing as close as you can to it, that's a terrific feeling!"

"Once," she says, "at interval, we were in the bar that looks over the water, and a big cruise ship was going out. It was all lit up, like a wall of light, floating past so close, and you felt you could put out your hand and touch it! Just to be there at that moment, it was —"

"Who's 'we'?"

"That was when I was still with my husband, Eric. You probably—"

"I never liked him," he says. "He was a bastard."

"But you were only—"

"Yeah. I knew a bastard when I saw one."

"He did have a—" You can't talk about these things to a kid, but he's waiting for the end of this sentence, at least. "A very bad temper."

"I'll bet he did." He's drawn his own conclusions.

When they get to her station, again he follows her to the door. She walks quickly down the platform, and as the train pulls out she sees him, a blur of white shirt, standing there.

∞

She really should drive, one of these Fridays.

Neither of them ever misses the train. The same carriage, always. Just the nod at first, the wait until he comes to sit beside her. Once a stout woman, hung around with shopping bags, came and settled herself down where he should sit. Alyson had to climb over her, find another seat. Then she saw him look for her, think she'd gone, catch sight of her—and light up. And knew, too late, that her face must reflect his.

After this, there's no pretending it doesn't matter. It matters. Well, why not? She's never thought to be friends with a kid, not after all these years. If you added them up, how many kids has she known? The total might be in the thousands. And not one a friend. But this is rather a special circumstance.

This Friday, she's saying goodbye. He's standing where he always stands, and the doors of the carriage are closing, the train about to move, when an old man, muttering, "Let me pass!" pushes by him.

"Don't!" she cries.

"Watch out!" yells Tom in the same moment.

The old fellow has already slipped, is falling into the space between platform and train. Tom's long arm flashes and his body follows, and somehow they're both propelled forward, the smaller man staggering, his fall broken and its course diverted, Tom sprawled heavily half-beneath him on the platform, at her feet.

The train's jerked and halted, the doors have opened again and the guard's running towards them. "What happened, mate?"

Tom, winded, looks up at him but can't speak. He rolls aside, disengaging himself from the victim, who yelps, "What do you think you're doing?"

"Is he all right?" The guard is a Sikh, and beneath his turban his face is ashen.

"You idiot! You could have killed me!"

"He saved your life, you silly old . . . you silly old I don't know what!" she cries.

Tom sits up. He seems to be very amused. He and the guard pull the old man to his feet, dust him down, feel his bones.

"It's no laughing matter," he grumbles.

An anxious face, blurry in the distance, cranes out of the window of the driver's compartment. Passengers gather, just curious, at the doors. A few people hover around them on the platform. One picks up Tom's bag, stuffing back into it some books that have spilled out, and hands it to Alyson. She hugs it to her chest.

"I'm calling an ambulance," says the guard. "And the police."

"Nothing's broken! I don't need any ambulance!"

"Regulations, mate." The guard's on firm ground now.

By the time it's all over, she's stopped shaking. The ambulance has gone, the train's gone, the police have made their notes, clapped Tom briefly on the shoulder, and gone, too.

"Looks like you've missed your yoga."

"This wasn't too relaxing." She knows her smile is crooked.

"It's the reaction," he says kindly. "I'll take you home."

"No, you won't! You'll go home!" This sounds rather vehement. "They'll worry if you're late."

"Nobody's there. Look," he says, "I feel a bit shook up myself. It's not far, is it? You could give me a drink."

She looks. He is rather pale now. "I suppose we could both do with one," she says doubtfully.

In her flat, his colour returns quickly. When she comes out of the kitchen with a bottle, a corkscrew and two glasses, he's standing by the fireplace, which is no longer really a fireplace, but a pleasant feature of these old rooms, taking everything in.

"Let me open it."

She lets him, resisting the temptation to echo his mother: only one for you.

"*Salute,*" he says.

"You were great," she answers, and sees him flush.

She sits on the edge of the sofa.

He stays where he is. His arm, the glass in his hand, rests easily along the mantelpiece. Does he know how graceful the effect is? He looks across at her and smiles.

It's her turn to ask. "Why are you smiling?"

"You were funny," he says. "'You silly old I don't know what!' It was nice of you not to swear at a poor old bloke."

Behind him, on the mantelpiece, there's a pot of angel's wings, huge and pale and delicately veined with green, of which she's very proud. They're tricky, they'll go too green if they don't get just the right amount of light. And a jumble of pictures. A careful jumble. That's how she wants it. A botanical drawing of a tomato plant, found in a junk shop on the highway. A Redouté print, *Rosa centifolia*, from her father, the rose-grower. Framed postcards. A detail, a lizard, from an aboriginal bark painting. The one just near his hand is a favourite thing from her time in London, from the endless hours she spent wandering hopefully from room to room in museums, waiting for her eye to light upon an object that would, even if only for a moment, take her mind off her predicament. Seeking solace, and finding it one rainy day in this. It's an Elizabethan miniature: *Young Man Against a Background of Flames*. There's the young man in his white shirt. A jewelled earring. And filling the small oval, flames, inexplicable.

She raises her eyes to his face.

"He did me a favour," he says. "Now I'm here."

She drinks the last of her wine in a single gulp, stands, takes
his empty glass, walks with the glasses in her hand to the
kitchen. "Time to go home," she says lightly.

She's putting the glasses in the sink when she senses that he's
right behind her. She knocks one over, leaves it, turns. Her face
is very near his chest. His shirt is smeared with dust, but she
smells fresh white cotton. A new shirt. He probably goes
through them fast. Grows out of them. She can feel the warmth
of his skin glowing through the shirt. His chest rises and falls too
rapidly. She can hear his breathing, it's the only sound in the
room.

"Aly," he says. "Let me kiss you."

Jesus. "No! No, Tom."

"Please."

"No! Stop this! Now." The authentic voice of the school-
teacher, not her own voice. Yes, her own.

He moves back uncertainly. His eyes don't move from her
face. He wants to know if she means it. "I mean it," she says.
They aren't grey, his eyes, they're blue after all. He reaches out,
not quickly this time but not tentatively either, and takes her by
both arms. His are slim, but very hard. She remembers this hard-
ness of muscle from the boys of her youth. It takes her breath
away.

He doesn't do anything. He just stands there, holding her. It can't last. She's not afraid of him, no never that. But if she doesn't think of something now, he'll try something stupid, it will get worse. She searches, and it comes to her that it's funny, really! How the kitchen is where his father always makes his moves!

Laughter will do it.

He gets out of the room. His elbow catches her metal coffee pot and it falls onto the floor, where it separates into its parts and rolls noisily away, but he seems not to notice.

He's already at the front door when she catches up with him.

"Tom! Please!" Now she's saying it.

The hurt in his face is unbearable. He didn't deserve this. He meant only to kiss her, he meant no harm. He tries awkwardly to push her away, but she takes his head in her hands. Oh God, what a mistake. Of all the mistakes she's ever made.

It's only a kiss. But it is the kiss she's wanted most not to end of all the kisses she's ever had.

There's more, of course there is. What did she expect? The awareness of his erection ignites in her blind panic. She wrenches herself away from him with all her strength.

Now it's both their breath, his and hers, loud in the room, and the width of the door between them.

"Go home!"

"No."

She puts out her hand, not to touch him, but to warn him, no further. "Oh Tom, please go home." And, amazing herself, she starts to cry.

He makes a sound, moves as if to take her in his arms and comfort her, but she shakes her head violently. It's clear where comfort leads.

She doesn't know any better than he does what to do next.

Finally, he says, "Would you . . . if I was older?"

All she can manage is: "What do you think?"

The words have an incredible effect on him. He blazes with happiness. "It's all right, then! But Aly, why not now?"

"You know why not!"

"But I've thought it all out!" he says.

Now she really laughs. Her mood seems to change as easily as his. "Oh, have you?"

"Yes. You see," he says eagerly, "I'm under age and everything. That's true. But who would know? And what's wrong with it? You didn't do anything, I did!"

"I did. I met you. Every Friday, didn't I?"

"Did you know?"

"I think so. I must have. Don't I!"

He stops where he is. Breathing hard still, but intent upon the logic of it. "It's not as if you're my teacher, or anything. There's no abuse of power. See?" How they love these words, kids. Abuse of power. Well, that's something.

"It's not legal," she says flatly. She thinks she couldn't stand without leaning against the door-frame. But this is very simple to say. "That's all there is to it."

He won't give up. "You wouldn't be taking my virginity," he says. "I've done it. Sort of," he adds honestly.

She finds this so endearing, now she's laughing and crying at the same time.

"Aly, don't cry. I can't stand it. Not if you won't let me—"

"No, I won't. I'm sorry."

"Who would ever know?"

"Go home. Just go home." She turns her face aside. After a long moment, he opens the door. "Don't forget your things."

She hears him cross the room to get his bag of books, and return. Then he's gone.

She slides to the floor and sits there with her head on her knees. When she gets up she feels stiff and about a million years old. And it goes through her brain and turns her insides to nothing: of all the dreadful mistakes. This is the one.

CHAPTER THREE

At first she expects to hear from Louise. She's all ready with an account of the accident, praise of Tom, his quick thinking, his reflexes, even mention of the single glass of wine before sending him home. Nothing wrong with any of that. The call never comes. He can't have said a word about it. But what if the police want to contact him for some reason? What if the old man has a heart attack, for example, and they need to confirm what happened? Or what if he wants to thank Tom, and— No, not likely. What if he gets it into his head to sue the railways, and they need witnesses? And then it comes out, and she herself hasn't said anything? What then? Should she? No. She waits. Nothing happens.

It's as if nothing did happen.

She can't believe they had that conversation. That they stood there, panting, and he actually tried, from beyond arm's length, to talk her into it! The nerve of the boy! And she was a participant in this ridiculous scene. She let it go on. No, it wasn't ridiculous. It was sweet. That's the word. Sweet. No, it's not. It was real. And what she said to him. *What do you think?* Oh, God. That was real, too.

Now she understands why people caught out in misdemeanours say, according to report, "I don't know what came over me." She doesn't know what came over her, and it's humbling to be a cliche. But he's a nice boy, a sensible boy, except for this one thing, and there's that reserved quality he has. He's not going to go telling all his friends, either. She's pretty sure of that, and it's some balm for her mortification.

Next Friday, she drives. She prays he had sense enough to get a different train. It hurts to think that he might have looked for her. No, surely he would know. He must realise that she couldn't. Couldn't possibly. Still it hurts.

She picks up the mail, tucks it under the flap of one of the folders full of essays that she's juggling, along with a carton of milk, a white paper bag containing two chocolate croissants, and the *TV Week*.

She makes a cup of tea and puts one of the croissants on a plate. They say chocolate has some mood-altering chemical in it. If you eat enough of it, maybe it has the same effect as yoga, for which she has no heart right now.

There's a note from her mother, enclosing a clipping about an orchid show. The telephone bill. It's the same as usual, almost to the cent. There's a plain square white envelope, addressed in a confident round hand. Not official, but not anyone she knows. No return address on the back. An equally plain white card inside. Black ink. An invitation to the ball, perhaps?

On the card is written only this: *From all wymmen my love is lent, Ant lyht on Alisoun.*

How did he get it? Perhaps one night they were talking over dinner, and Louise, to illustrate some point about language, jumped up to find this poem, the way she does, always putting her hand on the right book, opening it at the right page and an example the kids would likely remember. Middle English being her field, never missing a chance to teach. He's a quick study.

It's a love letter. She puts it back in the envelope, lays the envelope on the table. Takes up the envelope, opens it, reads the words again. How long is it since she's had one of these? This *is* sweet.

That's all it is. No reason to have taken it out and reread it, by the end of the night, countless times; or to have put it, finally, in the drawer of her bedside table where she keeps her great-grandmother's garnet brooch and so forth; or to have lain staring awake all night until it's light outside again. There has never been a love letter so perfect.

At five o'clock this morning, as she will every morning for a long time, she gets up and washes her face and goes out into the dewy greyness. She jogs, hating it, down to the park on the bay, and limps back uphill to the accompaniment of the magpies' carolling, until her foot begins to ache incessantly and the doctor says it's pronation. So then she starts driving to the pool at opening time. The same people are there every morning: the kids in the lanes set aside for training, the balding man with the wrestler's body and hairy chest, the wiry seventyish woman who can do a strong breaststroke forever. They're all good swimmers and their reasons for being here are no doubt wholesome. She tires easily, and then she does a lackadaisical backstroke and looks up at the brightening sky, and frankly she doesn't care if she ever gets fit or not.

Poetry is the hardest thing to teach. "The Wild Swans at Coole," for example. Nine-and-fifty swans. Unwearied still, lover by lover. In an essay handed in practically on the eve of the exams, and after she's only been talking about it for the whole year, they're ducks. Not the same thing, she writes in red, but the English staff get a chuckle out of it at the meeting, even Bill. Sometimes kids surprise you. Years ago, but it's stuck in her mind, a boy who was a surfer, with peroxided hair and those great knobs on his ankles that they get from being hit by the board, said to her, I like to read Donne when I'm stoked on a chick. I wonder by my troth, what thou, and I Did, till we lov'd? Probably. That was touching. She no longer makes an effort to keep up with their slang, though. You can't keep up with everything. Golden lads and girls all must, As chimney-sweepers, come to dust. They like that, for some reason.

There are only so many sick days you can take. In the end, you have to know how to work, how to teach through things. Colds in the head, deaths in the family. This.

It's not such a bad school. Compared to the school where she did her first practise teaching, as a student, it's a model institution. A boys' school, that was, when there were still more than a few, and the Headmaster was still called the Headmaster, and sat in his office with his cane—how was he getting away with it?—and you'd hear the swish, a predetermined number of strokes, four or six, like in cricket, on a boy's palm, as you passed. And the boy would come out, shaking his hand, tearful but more or less grinning, depending on who he thought was there to see. There was usually a queue, waiting their turn. The teachers were all men, and they had let themselves go, with their piles of dog-eared papers in which mice actually lived, their doughnut cushions, their pepper and salt shakers. They offered her all sorts of tips. If some clod's giving you trouble, they'd say, knowing she was having problems, and you don't want to send him to the Office, make him stand up in front with his hands on his head. Not too long, mind you. It can bring on a heart attack if he's got a weak heart, you never know. The place was a battleground. They didn't give her the swimming on sports afternoon because, they said, the kids tried to drown the last one. The last practise teacher, they meant. She thought her leg was being pulled, but apparently not. They sent her to the bowling alley. That school almost made her give up, but she didn't. She remembers what she taught there, too. Wilfred Owen. What passing bells for these who die as cattle? That quietened them down. And they went for it, the kids. They were hungry. That's probably why she made the mistake of keeping on.

She's rostered for swimming today, not that there's much to do with Mel in charge. It's better than basketball, where there's high-decibel screaming, a lot of it really foul, though they try to remember not to let you hear in case you feel obliged to crack down on it, or any of those things where you have to stand out in the middle of a hot field and just hope no-one gets clobbered on this particular afternoon with a stick or a ball.

Mel's surrounded by the usual gaggle of would-be non-swimmers. "Got my period!" they wail. "You silly girls!" she shouts at them.

"You think Olympic champions whinge about their silly periods? Swimming's good for you! If you've got a note, give it to me, otherwise get in the changing room, now, and I want to see you out in five minutes! No, three and a half. Get!"

At the end of the pool a group of long-legged big boys in little swim trunks are desultorily shoving each other towards the edge.

A wave of heat washes over her at the sight of them. And then another, but that's shame.

Mel's gesturing at her, and for an uncomprehending moment she thinks, stupidly, does it show? Of course not, it's only that her duty is being pointed out to her. She walks a little way towards the boys, stops short, says mildly, "You know the rule. No pushing." Unperturbed, they amble off. Well, there's one attempted tripping, but they know she's watching, so it doesn't come to anything.

The girls are hopping out of the changing room, from foot to foot on the hot cement, pulling down their swimsuits at the back with ineffectual tugs. Mel gets up on a low wall to read off her list. There's a bit of giggling and nudging in the group beneath her, and Alyson moves forward to see what's causing it. Oh-oh. Thick dark pubic hair, now at eye level, is curling out from under Mel's swimsuit. The girls are trying to catch Alyson's eye, inviting her to acknowledge the joke. Nothing to be done, except pretend to notice neither the disturbance nor Mel's lapse. Mel's not the kind of person to fuss over the bikini line, anyway. She probably wouldn't care.

Mel finishes the list, jumps nimbly down, sends them scattering in all the appointed directions. She pushes up the sunglasses that have slipped down her sweaty nose. To Alyson she says out of the side of her mouth, "We're being *particularly* silly today."

"Aren't we."

That night, she has an erotic dream. It's perfectly simple, it needs no interpretation. He asks her again, she gladly says yes. His body is whiter than it would be in real life, it's all more exquisitely tender than it ever can be in real life; she climaxes in her sleep. This is something unusual, and she wakes in a daze.

How has this happened to me? He has no idea what he's done.

In her first class of the morning, after Assembly, she intercepts a note. She's not sure where it's going, or who it's come from, but she moves between the tables in the soundless way she's mastered over the years, and takes it. There are the usual smothered snorts and murmurs, but also some pockets of utter silence. She knows better than to read it in front of them, be affronted, demand to know who wrote it, etcetera. "I'm going to throw this away," she says. "Now get on with it." This is only Year Eight. At the changeover, she does read it. It's an obscene note, an invitation of a kind, with drawings. It's not laughably obscene, nothing that'll raise a hoot in the staff room, nor creatively obscene. It's just plain obscene. Half of these kids are still really kids. And her only thought, before she tears it into confetti and throws it in the bin, is: it's not fair.

Her mother and stepfather are surprised when she turns up for Christmas.

Her mother proclaims her peaky, and she confesses to a hypothetical dose of flu. Each morning, oranges, pineapples, and bananas are buzzed up together in the blender for her, with a dollop of honey for extra energy. Thick slices of wholemeal toast, with pools of butter and globs of melon and ginger jam. Eggs soft-boiled according to her stepfather's special method, requiring the use of a stopwatch. Runny yolks, and whites barely set. This happens to be exactly how she likes them. She eats, and lets herself be carried along on the momentum of her mother's stories into the sunny morning.

"That's one of Fran's eggs," says her mother. "Did you ever see such beautiful yolks?" She saws vigorously at the end of the loaf. "They've settled down over there."

"The chickens?"

"The lot of them. Did I tell you? She had this flat built under the house for her son, you remember Derryn. Completely self-contained, he put in a Jacuzzi. Lovely boy, Derryn, I don't know if he was gay last time you were up?"

"Mum—"

"Well, he certainly is now, gone in for it in a big way, of course his father's not around any more, poor Ralph. So Derryn brought this young chap to live with him, and they seemed happy enough, or so he told his mother, but the upshot of it was, they fell out, and it was Derryn who left home. He went off to live with someone else, a young chap, and the other young chap was left there high and dry, and she didn't like to say anything, he was very upset. Then lo and behold, the other young chap takes up with— well, with another young chap, and then she's got two young chaps she hardly knows from Adam living under the house. It took a bit of getting used to. But it's all worked out, for the time being. She can go away for the weekend and they'll feed the chooks and lock them up from the foxes. Two Rhode Island Reds, two fancy yellowy ones, I forget their name. They can't do enough for her, they're both lovely boys. But the thing is, what's going to happen when Derryn wants to come back? It's his home."

"He should have thought of that," says Alyson.

"The heart has its reasons, he said to her."

"Very profound."

"You haven't had any bout of flu," says her mother. "This is to do with some love mix-up, isn't it? You never said you were coming. Not that we aren't glad to have you, my darling. Made my Christmas." She fields another piece of toast from the pop-up toaster.

"Doesn't that thing pop up too far?"

"Don't try and bamboozle me," says her mother, "I can see you're not saying. When you finish your breakfast, go down and talk to him about propagation. He's got his own methods. Oh, they're wonderful things! More than fifty thousand hybrids in the world, imagine that! He's going to call one after me, when he gets just the one he wants, he says."

Her mother, widowed by roses, is now in love with orchids, and her fond old husband surrounds her with beauty. The lavishness of her mother's life, the proliferation of colour, makes her feel all the more the leached-out quality of her own, but it warms, too. She returns with a back seat full of things: half a Christmas cake, jars of passionfruit butter and mango chutney, a sack of her stepfather's top-secret potting mix, a fine creamy *Cattleya* "Queen Sirikit," carefully shrouded in damp hessian ("She'll travel all right, she's tougher than she looks") and a head full of resolutions.

Most of these go for nothing when, soon after, she sees him in the street with a group of boys and girls. They're getting into a van, which presumably one of them is old enough to drive. He's wearing those long baggy khaki shorts that the boys wear, and carrying a guitar. One of the girls, the one in the shortest shorts, is Tiffany. Alyson hangs over her steering wheel as the lane she's in inches towards the intersection, praying not to be seen.

Louise calls to ask her to dinner. She refuses this invitation, and the next.

So the time goes on.

Louise is having a party. "We haven't seen you for *aeons*," she says.

Next, she'll be demanding to know why. There's no good reason, and what's the point, after all these months? "I'd love to come. I might have to leave early, though." Lie. "I might have to meet someone."

"Oh," says Louise."Why not bring him?"

"It's a bit complicated."

"I see," says Louise, meaningfully.

Perhaps it is the best way, after all.

It's a warm late summer evening, and the doors are open to the verandah. Lights skim across the water. Scented smoke rises from the barbecue. Tiger prawns attempt to curl on their skewers. That sharp note is fresh coriander. Toby, his hair glinting beneath the lanterns, is supervising the cooking, but he's not wearing any tacky apron. "Best time of year for a barbecue," he says.

"Pear salsa." Louise puts down a glass bowl and whisks away.

What's that? Alyson puts a surreptitious finger in the side of the bowl, licks it.

"I saw you!" says Katie

Brian is with her, looking bored. Alyson has never seen him looking anything but. And yet if Katie says his presence keeps her hormones in good nick, it must be true.

Louise brings a platter of tortellini. "We're being very eclectic tonight."

"Where are the kids?" asks Katie.

"Griselda's in charge of threading scallops on slivers of bamboo, Tom's not here."

"He has his own life now, I suppose," says Katie.

"He's got a little girlfriend, he's off somewhere with her."

"Legs up to here," puts in Toby. Brian perks up slightly.

"Little spindly legs," says Louise. "So coltish, and teetering on these incredible platform soles. I always think, oh, I hope she doesn't break her neck."

"It's understandable, they'd rather be with their own age." Katie wants children, or maybe she's given up by now, and the subject makes her lugubrious.

"She's a year younger. I did say he could bring her, but he didn't want to. Actually, I thought we might do something for his birthday, but he didn't want that either. We could have had all his friends, they could have had dancing downstairs, but he said—"

"These prawns are done, Louise."

He's over it now.

"Take them off, Toby! Not one second more!"

Alyson leaves as soon as she can. At the gate, she stops to find her keys. There's the sound of the party behind her, muted by the trees, and a short distance up the road, another, much noisier. Still, she hears a light movement in the branches above her head, and glances up. "He's not here," she says. "You knew not to depend on it, didn't you?"

This afternoon, another Friday, her car breaks down on the way home. Right on the highway. She pulls onto the shoulder, gets out, lifts the bonnet. Flames spurt up from the battery. She jumps back. It's really on fire!

A delivery truck stops. The driver runs up. "Got an extinguisher?"

If I had, I'd be using it, she wants to say. Do you think I'm that stupid? Then again, I'm stupid enough not to have an extinguisher. "No, have you?"

"Nope. Oughter have one."

In the end, there's quite a crowd, but nobody's got an extinguisher, so the fire just burns itself out in the glare of the afternoon sun.

She rides in the tow truck to the garage, and calls a taxi.

In the middle of a busy shopping centre the taxi rams into the back of a car that's edging jerkily out of an awkward parking space. The driver turns to Alyson, who's been thrown roughly forward, not having done up her seat belt, and spits out: "You seen that! Bloody woman!" Before she can think of what to say, the person in question comes storming up to the window.

"Couldn't you see I was backing!" she shrieks. She takes a closer look. "You ignorant foreigner!"

He gets out, slamming the door, which they usually hate. "Look at the damage you done to my cab, silly bitch! How come they give you a license, you got no brain!"

Alyson rests her head against the side window, closes her eyes. The battle rages. Racism vs. sexism. I can't stand it, she thinks. She gathers up her things, opens the door quietly, and sneaks away, her fare unpaid.

She trudges all the way home, on foot.

He's there, waiting for her, sitting quietly on the stairs.

He stands up, puts out a hand to take her books. Mutely, she finds her key, opens the door.

Her mouth is horribly dry. "I need a glass of water," she says.
He stays by the kitchen door. "You know I'm sixteen," he says.
She drinks the water down, refills the glass. "I hear you didn't want a party."

"Why should I want a party? That's not the point."

No, it isn't.

This silence is very long.

"I think we'd better just do it," he says.

She rinses the glass, places it neatly in the rack, walks past him into the living room, hesitates.

"In the bedroom, Aly," he says, "properly." And after a moment, follows her.

The mistake's already made, and once will be enough, after that he'll lose interest. I only need this once.

Unbuttoning his shirt, unbuckling his belt, unzipping him. Nothing has ever made her feel before such a concentration of time. It happens in another dimension. He's brought a pocketful of condoms. Dear God. He kneels, her face in his hands. "You won't be sorry, you'll see," he whispers.

"I don't care! Oh Tom. Please."

The life in which she watched people standing in the street screaming abuse at each other was another life. The life in which she had no idea what it would really be like to have Tom, the life in which she knew only enough of him to cause her pain—that was another life, too.

She had no idea then what it would be to know his body whole, just this once. To put together all of him that she's kept so long in memory, and all she never thought to know. All of him beautiful—his penis in its delicate sheath of skin, his tongue, his eyelashes. His very breath, the quickness and the slowness and the warmth of it.

She had no idea, for all her imagining, of what it would be like to hold him as he loses himself in her, after a careful beginning apparently in accordance with a long-cherished plan, in a racking jolt that does nothing, it turns out, to dent his confidence. Or of what it would be like to feel herself come, beyond all power to have it otherwise, in a welter of helpless sobbing that brings with it no humiliation, only caresses that restore to her, just this once, smiles of an innocence she would have thought lost forever.

He lies back, stretches the way he did that first day on the train. Lightly, she kisses his stomach, lets her lips move where they want to, down among sticky, light-brown curls, breathes in the scent of him, overlaid with her own, surprises even now a gentle twitch that makes them both laugh. She rests her cheek on his smooth brown thigh, and thinks, idiotically, I am in heaven. Then he reaches down and pulls her up, settles her against his chest. He seems to know exactly how he wants her, his arm around her, the other hand here and there, finding out. He ascertains the SPF of the sunblock she uses. You've got to be careful, Aly, when your skin's so pale and you've got these moles. Yes, Tom, she says. Oh God, this happiness.

"I've always had these thoughts about you," he tells her, in between blowing soft breaths into her hair.

"Always?"

"Well, since I started to have these thoughts. I always thought you were beautiful."

"Even when my hair was mousy?"

"I said always."

"I had a dream about you."

"A dream? You mean one?"

"Mostly I day-dream."

"I do that, too. But dreams about you. You know." He laughs. "I couldn't count."

"You're sixteen." It doesn't seem strange to say it.

"I don't know how I waited."

"I didn't know you were waiting."

"You thought I'd given up?" He looks down at her incredulously. "You just don't know enough about me yet."

"I'm learning." A stab, self-inflicted. To speak as if there's all the time in the world! It's the opposite. Time, that seemed endless when this was impossible, now that they're here in her bed, is ending.

"One more," he says. She turns her face up from his chest to look into his.

"You have to go home soon."

His lips bent to her breast, he recites: Louise, evening lecture, Toby clearing up the week's work so he says, Griselda training.

Yes. Yes. She can't manage the words for him to hear, but he knows.

When he stands up to dress, she pulls him towards her again, meaning only to kiss the vulnerable hollow below the hip bone, white, just where his swimsuit stops. His head lifts and he makes a single sound, between a gasp and a moan. And the thrill that runs through her, a needle of incredible fineness shuddering down an unsuspected vein, straight from scalp to curling sole, for this instant frightens the life out of her.

One more, one more.

In the end, she buttons his shirt for him with slow fingers. He zips up his trousers. These grey trousers are his school uniform. Her stomach gives a quick lurch. Too late for that. It's done. She has never felt more tenderness for any human being. Now all that remains is to accept that this is all that can ever be, and find a way to go on.

"Kiss me, Tom," she says.

"Stay there," he tells her. "Stay in bed, I like how you look there." At the bedroom door, he stops, comes back. "You're not sorry, are you?" He's not flirting with her, it's a question.

"You know I'm not."

He pulls away the sheet, she grabs for it, wraps it hard around herself. "Go."

"It'll be easier if you give me a key."

She sits there with the sheet clutched to her and her mouth open.

"For next Friday," he explains. "I feel a bit obvious out there, if you're held up. The lady upstairs gave me a funny look this afternoon."

"You are practical," she says at last. "There's a spare in the drawer."

He opens the drawer, and there's the square white envelope, with his own writing on it.

He smiles, finds the key, slips it in his pocket. "Did you like what I wrote?"

"Yes. Very much."

"It's in a dictionary of names," he says. "In the library. I looked up yours. Your way of spelling's in there, it's fifteenth century, did you know that? I just wanted to see your name. I looked at it over and over. Hundreds of times. You would have thought I was crazy."

So that's how it was. The idea all his own.

"No," she says. "No, I wouldn't."

"I love you, Aly. I know you won't say it to me. You wouldn't want to encourage me too much. Don't worry. I can wait."

I'm not as brave as you, Tom, she thinks as the front door clicks shut. You know that too.

She sleeps, wakes up about midnight, disoriented, to the sound of voices calling "Goodnight! Goodnight!" down in the street. Switches on the light. There are her clothes on the floor, bedclothes scattered and twisted. And falling back on the pillow, heart thumping, she knows it wasn't true what she swore to herself, that she only needed this once. It seems almost like sacrilege, to have thought it.

A week. No, some hours are already gone. Count the hours. This is how to get through the week.

It is possible.

And then there are the years.

CHAPTER FOUR

"*I* think we should go away next weekend," he says casually, sitting on the side of the bed, pulling on a grey sock.

If I didn't feel so lethargic, she thinks, I'd get out of bed and kneel down and put on his socks for him. I'd kiss his feet first. His feet are too big, like a puppy's feet, too long. She sits up. "*What?*"

'We can't always just be like this, Aly."

Just?

"They're going away," he says. "Down to Wollongong, Zelda's got a competition. Leaving me at home to finish my project, which I've already done. All I have to do is leave food for the cat. We can go."

She is dumbfounded. We have to be like this! It's all I ever think of, these few hours, here, everything else in the world shut out. Safe. He's looking at her, waiting for an answer. "It wouldn't be safe, Tom."

"They're going South," he says. "We go West. The Blue Mountains. Katoomba."

"Katoomba! We could see anybody. They could see us."

"What are the odds? It's a very small risk, Aly. And it's better than being seen in a really out-of-the-way place, if it comes to that."

She shakes her head. Doesn't he get it? And then she gets it. "What you want is a date!"

"Right!" he says. "And we can't go out round here yet, I know that!"

That heart-breaking eagerness of his. That "yet." He thinks I'm his girlfriend. "This is different," she says gently. "It's got to be. Don't look so stubborn. Think about it." Then she thinks, this isn't enough for him now! If I don't—

"It's not that it's not enough," he says, and she makes a slight movement that must tell him he's read her mind. It probably wasn't too hard, not for a quick learner like Tom. "It's everything. But there's a world. We've got a right."

A right. What right? "What if they call?"

"They'll leave a number. I'll call them. Then they'll know I'm OK, so what's the difference?"

This is awful. "We might have an accident on the road. What then?"

"We won't," he says.

∞

So far, so good. No accident. It hasn't been a good drive. He hasn't enjoyed it at all. He's been fidgeting beside her, slumping in the seat, crossing his legs wide, putting a foot up on the dashboard, sighing and groaning, and it's been all she could do not to say anything. Stop it this minute. Won't tolerate this behaviour. Something like that. He thinks he should be driving.

But now, at the motel, he comes to life. He's half out of the car before it stops. "I'll go and get the key."

"Tom—you can't!" Does he think they give keys to kids?

"Are they going to ask? I'm tall." Great. The whole point of a motel is so you don't get noticed. "And Aly, I'm paying."

"You've got money?" They stopped once on the way, at an old-fashioned cafe, and he bought her a vanilla milkshake. She didn't think anything of it. "For this?"

"Yes, I've got money," he says, exasperated. "I've had jobs." Damn it, his savings. He gets out. "Just wait here."

And he comes back with the key.

As soon as they're in the room, she forgets everything. She's as elated as he is. He swings her off her feet, tosses her on the bed, falls on top of her.

"Tom," she says, "No condom, it's all right."

"You're supposed to," he says.

"You—" She takes a deep breath. "You've never done it without, right? And I—" No need to say, I hadn't done it at all, not for years. "I'm on the pill now. I give blood, I've been tested. It's all right. As long as . . . as long as it's—" This explanation is getting too long.

"Monogamous," he finishes briefly for her. "Got it." His hand's under her skirt, urgently tugging down her tights and panties. As urgently, she releases him from his jeans. He's radiant to the touch with a heat that's like no other, and spilling over.

He couldn't stop, now. Oh, me either, I'd die. Everything else stops. Pompeii. Ancient people, bodies joined together. Like this, like we are. A volcano! They didn't hear a thing. Lucky, these mountains are very very old. Tom, on the other hand—

"Aly. Look at us!" He just gets the words out, on a caught breath.

It's setting a bad example, but it's beautiful.

Dinner at a small hotel, one they can walk to from here, is not a success. Fresh-painted wooden curlicues beckon, but inside the place seems to be a repository of unsaleable Victoriana from a long-defunct antique shop, and the dining room is three-quarters empty. The waiter's not unversed in the ways of weekend travellers, he's just not very quick off the mark. After Alyson orders for herself, he begins to say, "And what would your—"

and stops, just in time. There's something about them. The word "son" hangs suspended over the table like a dusty chandelier.

Tom's been looking at the wine list, and he orders a bottle of a chardonnay that Toby bought a case of on one of his Hunter Valley forays. "And a bottle of mineral water," she adds hastily. What's the law on serving minors anyway? The wine is brought, and she makes a stiff little gesture towards Tom's glass.

"You taste," she mutters.

With a flourish that's uncalled for, the waiter pours, then retreats to the back of the room, where he lifts an eyebrow at a woman in black.

"Well, here we are," says Tom, touching his glass to hers.

Here we are.

The hardest part is later. When he calls his parents, the conversation is minimal, but she gets up and goes into the bathroom. As she passes, he says, his voice perfectly natural, "Just going to bed." Who'd be a parent? He's turned away and doesn't look at her.

And when she comes out, he says only, "It's worth it, Aly."

She wakes up first. His head on the pillow beside her. The brown in his hair, underneath, is darker than she knew. She touches it with a finger. It's slightly damp with sweat. He turns over, revealing one flushed cheek, like a child. Please don't wake up, Tom, not yet, I want to look at you. His long hand curves over her breast. Her arm is going numb, but she doesn't move. Someone shoves a tray in the serving hatch, with the mini-packs of rice bubbles on it that she used to wait so eagerly for as a kid. A moment later a newspaper is shuffled under the door. He opens an eye.

"Your eyes are grey today."

"I think they're usually grey in the morning."

Mist swirls round the window. As it clears, the outlines of trees and bushes appear, and there are bright parrots hanging upside down from seed rings in the branches. He sits in the one wooden armchair, watching, his fingers practising imagined chords on his knee. She combs her hair, damp from the shower, and dresses, watching him.

"You sit here, Aly."

"What are you doing?"

From one of the pockets of his backpack, he's taken a camera. It's not a beginner's camera. He certainly doesn't want for anything. "What does it look like?"

"The birds?"

"No, you." He's turned out onto the bed several lenses and filters, and now he's screwing something off and something else on. "This one's for later, so the blue won't be too intense with colour film, that's a problem up here. Everything comes out looking like a postcard if you're not careful."

"Tom, you can't."

"Why not?"

"We're not supposed to be here."

"And who's going to see it?" She shrugs. "You don't think they go through my things?" he says. "Come on, Aly! Now look a bit—yeah, a little to the left."

Looking to the left, she thinks, I can't stop this any more than I could not be here.

He unfolds a tripod, sets up the camera. Then, to her surprise, he seizes her, and sits down in the chair with her on his knee, so that when the flash goes off, she's struggling and laughing. So he sets it up again, and this time he stands soberly behind her. Like one of those old wedding photos, she thinks.

"Should be in sepia," he says.

The mist still fills the valleys, but in the cold sun the mountains are as blue as they've ever been. He lopes along the paths, and she's glad every time he stops to take a picture of a tree-trunk or a rock. Sometimes he has to change a lens so he can get a shot of some lichen or a leaf lying on the path, and then she can catch her breath. Once she has to say, "Slow down a bit."

"I forgot," he says apologetically. "My legs are longer."

He's not being kind, he probably doesn't even realise that twenty years make a difference. It's not the sort of information you've really internalised by sixteen. You hear it, you know the theory of it, but it's like a swear-word in a foreign language: it has meaning, but no emotional weight.

It's not that she's feeling old yet, not at all, and it's not as if she's ever been a great strider up and down mountains, but she recognises the loss, whenever it was, of that careless sense of infinitely renewable energy he has now.

He bounds down a high step cut in a rock, and then in a comically courtly way puts up a hand for her, but he doesn't let her find a foothold when she's down, he pulls her into his arms. At that moment a family rounds the next bend in the path. She twists away from him. Mother, father, and two little girls. They pass, averting their eyes. It's no-one who could possibly know them, not that the thought seems to cross his mind. When they're out of sight, he takes up where he left off.

They hear water hissing, and below them the fall of it tumbling from rock to rock. The path further down is mossy and fern-fringed, and before they can see anything but trees their faces are misted with fine droplets blown off the cascades by the breeze that lingers round them even on this still, cold morning.

Looking up, she knows these falls. When she was his age, six-teen, she came to the mountains with a group of friends, all girls, and the path at the top, she can't make it out from here, was where they walked. A sunny day, a sketchy map of the mountains with the different falls marked on it, Bridal Veil and so on. The Victorian imagination was fairly predictable, but she likes these old names still. For some reason they'd left the path—God, the things kids do. They were scrambling down the side of the stream, to the point where it launched itself into the valley. Perhaps they wanted to look over, it must have been something insane like that. She lost her footing on a slippery rock, and fell, into the shallow water that skimmed over glassy sandstone. Screaming as the others screamed she slipped far towards the edge. There was a pointed rock, and her clothes and then her hands caught it, and there she clung, almost at the drop. One of her friends, someone she hasn't seen for many years, who might be anywhere now, inched down the side and, kneeling, extended a hand. It wasn't only the hand—it would have been possible to crawl to safety without it if she only could have moved—it was the words, come on, come on, that let her do it. She went home, dried by the sun, with only a grazed leg to explain, and never told her parents, never.

Tom's climbed up on the wet boulder behind the falls. It's the wetness, the slipperiness that makes her fear now, though there is no drop. You could at worst break an ankle falling into the pool where her body might that day have been found lurching from rock to rock, caught in the eddies. Still she can't move. Come on, Aly, he calls above the sound of the water. She takes his hand and clambers up.

By the end of the morning, he's hungry, but now she's getting nervous. What if his parents are already on their way home? "They won't be," he promises, but it does no good.

"Let's go."

They're walking back to the car with the large quantity of food he feels in need of for the journey ("The mountain air," she says, but he replies, "I generally eat this much for lunch") when she catches sight of something in a shop window, backtracks to make sure. "Mountain devils!"

She's never known the botanical name of the plant they're made from. She thinks of it as the mountain devil bush. Each split twig has a three-pointed thorn on top for muzzle and horns; add a few details, dress it with scraps, and it's a doll. Here, in the midst of a selection of old-fashioned souvenir things, crocheted koala tea-cosies, ashtrays with ceramic gum-nuts, there are still just a few mountain devils. But no-one picks native plants any more, and surely it wouldn't be profitable to grow them just for this? Old stock, perhaps, or the estate of a deceased mountain devil craftsperson? "I remember when I first came up here with my parents," she says. "It was misty, just like it was this morning. We walked, quite far. I was only four. We made our voices echo over the valley. And my father bought me a ballerina mountain devil. She seemed taller than these, then. I've still got her in a box at home."

"Wait here." He goes into the shop, and a moment later appears behind the window, pointing. Then he reaches in, and picks out a devil with pipe-cleaners dyed red for arms and tail, a devil cloak of red felt, and a twig pitchfork. He holds it out to her in his palm, enquiring. She nods. He comes out with a small brown paper bag, and gives it to her.

"She's got to have a partner," he says.

He's developed the photos himself. "I didn't know you had a darkroom."

"Behind the garage." He waits impatiently while she looks at them. "The black and white's more interesting, don't you think? You can do more with it."

"The trees and rocks are good. Really."

"What about these?"

"I'm afraid to look. I hate pictures of myself."

"Why would you hate them?" he asks, puzzled.

There she is, on his knee. There's the serious one. And herself alone. And now she knows. She didn't hate pictures of herself until she married Eric. That was when it began. "Smile!" he would say, and later, irritably, "Why can't you relax in front of the camera? Look, you spoiled this one. You'll just have to learn." She never did.

These pictures are different. This eye is a loving eye. "Can I keep them?"

"Yes, you keep them," he says.

The one of them both, the laughing one, she puts in a frame by the bed. Sometimes when he's not there she finds herself standing in front of it, incredulous. This is me. This is him.

CHAPTER FIVE

The older woman is supposed to be the teacher. Alyson would be happy never to have to teach anyone anything again. The last thing she wants is to teach Tom, to replicate the diligence of the classroom when they're in each other's arms. And she has nothing to teach him. What she learned from her marriage of the uses of the body she wants only to forget. Nothing she thought she knew before this means anything now. There has never been anything like this of kindness, sweetness, and yes, cleverness. There has never been anybody like Tom, nobody who ever wanted to know the things about her that he does and delights in, nobody willing to reveal more of himself. She's learning about Tom, and he is endless.

She simply has to stay out of the way.

"Louise is going to ask you to dinner," he says one Friday.

"I can't go."

"No," he says. "We can't be looking at each other in front of them. It's not like that."

It's nothing at all like that.

"Sixteen years, nine months. Not that long now," he says, his hands clasped behind his head on the pillow.

"What happens then?" she enquires lazily, nuzzling across his chest and into his armpit, where there's light fawn-coloured hair.

"That's when I can get my learner's permit."

"For what?"

"For a motorbike."

"You're getting a motorbike?" she exclaims, alarmed.

"Louise doesn't like it, either." He grins. "Don't be like that. You have to do a course, you know. You learn all the safety stuff. And you can only ride a 250 for the first year. Toby says I can have a Honda."

"Then Toby's a fool."

"Come on, wouldn't you like to ride pillion?"

"No."

He doesn't say, then I'll have to get a girl who will. Even to tease.

Sixteen years and nine months is when it happens. It had to happen. Not at once, no. It's taken this long.

He's done his two-day course, at the earliest possible moment.

He's got his learner's permit and his bike. She hasn't seen it yet. And here he is, late Saturday night, standing at the door she's answered in her old terry bathrobe, with his helmet in his hand. Surely he's never ridden before in the dark?

"I didn't want to scare you," he says. "So I rang the bell."

She looks at his tense face, and feels sick. "They know."

"It's my fault. I kept one."

"One of the photos."

"Just of you."

Fingers to her lips, she thinks about the photo. It's perfectly respectable, she's fully dressed. In a fluffy sweater, with a turtle-neck up to her chin. But her hair is damp. From the shower. Where, as it happens, they had made love. Where Tom— Furthermore. In every one of those pictures there was just the smallest corner. A shadow. But unmistakably a bed.

He walks past her into the room, shuts the door. "I haven't said anything. I beat them on the bike. But I think they'll be here pretty soon. I'm sorry, Aly."

"You're not to blame."

"I won't let them tell you that you are," he says. He puts the helmet carefully on a chair.

"A very handsome helmet," she says.

"That's it, Aly. Stay cool. What can they do?"

This is bravado.

I have to change out of this tatty robe, she thinks, suddenly frantic. The bell rings. No time for anything.

It's a long time since she's seen them, but that alone doesn't account for the fact that they look like strangers.

Eric always spoke admiringly of Toby's skills as a prosecutor. She could never see it. Now she does. This must be the face he uses.

Louise is a Fury.

She doesn't speak. She can't speak, thinks Alyson. But she wants to. Her eyes are unnaturally wide, protuberant with the effort to speak.

"What's this all about, Alyson? I'm giving you a chance to tell us. Now." Toby rounds on Tom, pointing a finger. "You keep your mouth shut!"

Tom ignores him, turns to Louise: "You went through my things! You had no right!"

He's diverting their attention from her.

"It could have been drugs, anything! Your mother had every right!"

"Drugs?" He's taken aback, but Alyson sees how it was. Lateness, distractedness, secretiveness. Not like Tom, for all his reserve and independence. Warning signs.

"No right!" Louise's tongue is freed, but this is not Louise's voice. It's dry and cracked. "No right! I have the right, and I have the responsibility! You think you've got the right to deceive us? This is despicable!"

"I was supposed to come and tell you? Or Aly was?" There's a pause while each of them imagines that scene. "I don't call it deception," he says. "I call it privacy."

Toby explodes. "Don't talk to me about privacy, you randy little twerp! Aren't we entitled to anything? We're only the ones who keep you! And so bloody well, too!"

"Is that what's bothering you? You mean you own me?"

This is classic, thinks Alyson, her hands at the neck of her robe, trying to keep it closed. Except for me. They'll get to me soon.

"How do you think you got that motorbike outside? Tell me that!"

"Take back your motorbike."

"Don't be bloody stupid!"

"I want to know— how long— this has been going on." Between words, Louise takes sharp, shallow breaths.

"I was sixteen." He doesn't say, I waited. That's none of their business.

"You think you can do anything when you're sixteen? Including fucking a fat witch more than twice your age!"

Toby, looking to Alyson as if for confirmation, looks quickly away again.

"You shouldn't talk about Aly like that," says Tom. "I won't forget it. But you're getting the idea. And it wasn't her, it was me." Alyson closes her eyes, and opens them to see Louise's on her. No-one else has ever looked at her like this.

"It wasn't her. Oh, no. And what would you know about it?"

He's unmoved by the contempt in her tone. He has a single point to make, and he's concentrating on it. "I'll tell any judge you like. I was sixteen. If you go after Aly, you're wasting your time."

Isn't someone going to say, let's try to be civilized about this, or: what can we do now?

Louise's gaze ranges round the room, searching. She fixes on something. At first Alyson thinks it's herself, and grasps the neck of her robe tighter, but whatever it is, it's behind her. "My God!" breathes Louise.

On the mantelpiece are the mountain devils: the ballerina brought out of the sleep of years, in her scrap of shabby white tulle, and her partner, the red devil. Tom likes to fool around with them. Sometimes he bends their pipe-cleaner arms and makes them hug or dance. Last time he was here he left them lying down, the ballerina on top of the devil, their thorny muzzles touching. She found them like that after he'd gone, and laughed, and left them there, where they are now, lying in front of her pictures: the tomato, the rose, the young man.

Louise lunges at the tableau, grabs up the dolls, crushes them in her fist, and throws them, with a sound, "Ugh!" and all the force she can manage, into the empty fireplace. She turns, takes a furious step, seems to be making for the bedroom, as if bent on a quest for more evidence.

Tom stands in front of her. "Get out!" he roars.

Toby moves between them, puts his face menacingly in Tom's. "Don't you dare!" At the same time, with an outflung arm, he too blocks Louise's path, but as if to shield her from some horror within.

There is no horror, there never was.

Out of the blue, a memory comes to her. A sunny garden, an inflatable wading pool, two naked children, and the voice of a younger Louise, earnest, didactic, innocent: "I never stop them touching themselves, Alyson. Children do have a right to express their sexuality." She feels hysterical giggles bubbling up her windpipe, threatening to burst out of her mouth. What will Tom think of her then?

As rapidly as it's risen, the hysteria evaporates.

Louise's face is crumpled in shock. And shame. For which, thinks Alyson, though Tom may be forgiven, I never can be. "Alyson." This is the first time she's spoken to me. This is Louise's own voice, though broken with anguish. "Didn't you— even once— think how I'd feel?"

Her face must show the answer.

No, not once.

"You're coming home with us," says Toby to Tom. "You can leave the bike."

"I'm not."

"You haven't got any choice, son!" Son. Until now, too traditional a form for Toby and his son.

"That's exactly what I have got. I'm sixteen."

Speak.

"You've had your scene," she says, not letting go of the robe. Her own voice sounds to her as if it's been years since she's used it. "But this is my place. If Tom wants to stay, he stays. And you both—please go home now."

"If he stays, he needn't bother to come home again!"

"Don't say things you don't mean, Toby." Now I'm doing it, piling up cliches. And we were educated to think a cliche was the worst thing in the world.

Louise, openly weeping, puts out a hand to Tom, touches his arm. "Oh, darling."

Tom is as white now as a moment ago he was red. He stands still, unrelenting.

And I thought I had most to lose.

He picks up the devils, straightens their pipe-cleaner arms, smooths the ballerina's skirt with his forefinger. "There's not a lot you can do to a mountain devil," he says. He replaces them on the mantelpiece, but standing, chastely, arms around each other's waists.

She gets out a bottle of sherry, pours two glasses.

"It's not that sweet stuff, is it?"

"It's very dry."

Looking down at the glass between his hands on the table, he asks, "Was this the worst night of your life?"

"No." How to answer? "That was when my husband first hit me." Actually, he didn't hit me, he took me by the hair and bashed my head against the corner of the refrigerator. She looks across the table. He doesn't ask, he wouldn't. He knows enough, and he knows it distresses her to speak of it. And to tell him everything, to arouse all his tenderness and protectiveness of her, to distress him on account of the past, would be unforgivable because so utterly futile.

After a while, she says, "Was it yours?"

"No. That was the night Grandad Daniel died on the tennis court, in front of me." She'd forgotten this, the massive coronary on the tennis court. "He liked to play when it was cooler. I liked it, too—the lights, the insects, the darkness all round. He'd just sent a serve right past me. And then he fell down. But now I'm here with you. So how bad can it be?"

In bed, at first she thinks, I can't. Not after that. But they do, tentatively at first, and then with a kind of solemn exhilaration. There is one point where she spares the briefest thought for Louise, lying awake all night as she must be. Aly, he says. Aly, my Aly. And the thought is gone.

In the morning, she's drained, and he is quiet. They drive over to his parents' place and she waits out the front in the car while he gets his things.

Griselda comes out and leans an elbow on the open window. "I've got to be honest with you," she says.

"There's no need, Griselda. If you don't mind."

"I think it's gross," says Griselda, undeterred. "I'm mad too, make no mistake." She bites at a hangnail, spits it out. "But it's not like anybody died. You'd think it was. I mean, I said to them, get over it. He's not dead."

"That was helpful."

Tom returns with an armful of clothes, tosses them in the back seat. "Make yourself useful," he says to Griselda. "Go and get my camera and stuff from the darkroom."

"You can't tell me what to do. Especially now."

He looks at her, and she goes.

The car fills up. Boxes of books and papers and CDs. His computer, and its scanner and printer. The guitar and the lute. "I'll hold these," he says.

"Can I have your room?" asks Griselda.

"If you promise to do what I asked you, you can have it."

"How many times a week?"

"Every second night. No forgetting."

"Strawberry, right?"

His possum. How could he not have been thinking of her? Being Tom.

"Tom?" she says desperately. "Don't make decisions now."

"I'm never coming back," he says.

"Did you see them?"

"No."

"But they're there?"

"In their studies."

"Hadn't you better?"

"No."

"Not much point," agrees Griselda. "Maybe later." Suddenly, she flings herself at him. "See what you've done, Aly!" she sobs over his arm.

"I don't want to hear that from you." He sounds like Toby.

"I just hope you're happy!"

There's Louise, on the upstairs verandah. "Griselda!"

"Go," he tells her. She goes, as fast as she does everything, and Louise disappears.

Alyson tries to start the car, and stalls it twice, but eventually they drive away.

He has the guitar between his knees, and the lute in his arms, somehow. "You know what a vihuela is?" he asks her. "It's a cross between a guitar and a lute. Sixteenth-century Spanish pops. If I ever have the money, I'll get one made."

"It'd save a lot of trouble when you move."

"That's what I mean," he says. "Thank Christ I gave up the piano. It's all right, Aly, it's all right. Please. Just watch the road."

Rather obviously, he puts out his shaving things in the bathroom. She makes room for his clothes in the wardrobe. He hangs them up, including his school trousers and blazer. Much too late now, for the feeling in the pit of her stomach. His shirts are all white, and all his non-school trousers, even blue jeans, fashionably cut. It's a look. It goes with the hair, short back and sides and long at the top, parted almost in the centre, and it's reminiscent of photos her mother has of her grandfather as a young man. When she tells him, he nods in satisfaction. It's a retro look, he says.

There's a table in the small second bedroom where she's been keeping her sewing machine and other things infrequently used, and here he sets up his computer. He's got software for everything. This is CAD, he says, computer-aided design, a special one for drawing buildings. But he also shows her the cloth-bound notebook in which he draws the old-fashioned way, by hand. He's got pages and pages of architectural details from Italy: archways, ornate hinges, window frames. Some, here and there, are washed with delicate colour. "This is where I kept your photo," he says regretfully. "Between these two pages. Because of the flowers in the carving."

"Where is it now?"

"Louise tore it up." She knows nothing about the scene before the scene, but it's all too possible to imagine.

She puts down the notebook. "Louise was a good friend to me." She's thinking of when she finally made up her mind to leave Eric. The animal! said Louise. Don't try and make excuses for him. His childhood, his complexes! Feel free to hate him. That was good advice.

Tom says bluntly, "You don't have to feel so bad. She did accuse Toby of sleeping with you. But I always knew it was rubbish," he adds hastily.

"It was rubbish!"

"I said I know. He's got hair in his ears. I'm just trying to make you feel better."

"Thanks," she says. "I think."

"She's not a bad mother." He's biting his lip. Now he thinks he's been disloyal.

"Of course she's not, Tom."

"Not only the basics, everyone knows she's good at all that. She's not slow on the uptake like some of them are, and she never embarrassed me."

"That's important." Louise and I can never again speak as we used to, she thinks. There's no way, now.

"Absolutely," he says. "She was never like— For instance, I'd go to the place of this kid you don't know, and his mother'd come out and say, 'What do you think of my new blouse?' She meant her tits. Every time, something like that. Or she'd make it so she could sort of touch you. I felt sorry for him." He reflects. "It's not uncommon, you know."

"Really."

"I often . . . appreciated Louise." He brushes the cover of the notebook with his fingertips. "She gave me this. It's the best Italian paper, Fabriano. It takes watercolour beautifully. Aly, last night, what she said. What she did. She was never like that before."

Later, in bed, he says, "I suppose Dad did put the hard word on you."

"Oh, Tom, it was nothing."

"I know what it was. He does it to all the women, the nice-looking ones, but there's no special type he likes or anything. He's given Mum a bad time, Aly. She wouldn't let on, she's tough. Sometimes I think—I suppose I shouldn't—she seems hard, compared to you. But it's got to have been bad. You know Katie? Mum caught him kissing her in the kitchen. Zelda was there, she told me. Said she wasn't totally against it."

"*Katie* wasn't?"

"No. Well, I don't reckon old Brian'd be up to much, do you? Though Zelda likes to keep out of his way."

"*Brian's* way?"

"Especially when she was younger. He was always trying to get her by herself. Really irritated when I tagged along. It was always, like, Zelda, give me a tour of your doll's house, Tom, haven't you got anything else to do? That sort of thing's a symptom," he explains. "You know the doll's house?"

"Your grandmother's?"

"It's a perfect Federation model, must have cost a packet when it was new. I renovated it for Zelda, put in a music room and a pool. Without destroying its essential character. I was more into it than she was. Anyway, now it's all karate, and she's not so shy any more. So Brian's no problem."

"Good."

"Aly? About Toby. Don't think I'm going to be like him, because I'm telling you, I'm not. I don't want to be. I won't be. Even though I tried to kiss you in the kitchen."

That's what he wanted to say.

∞

How does he know so much? At his age, I thought as little as possible about my parents' lives. What Mum and Dad might know about anything was nothing to do with me. I'd go skating with a boy, round and round to rock music, avoiding the bright red patches on the ice where someone had fallen, his arm around my waist, or to a party where we'd get all sweaty close dancing, and someone else's parents, ciphers, would be hovering outside the darkened room. At home, he'd kiss me, he'd push me up against the trunk of the tree near the front door and put his hands under my blouse, but the cold in winter or the mosquitoes in summer would drive us inside, and then Mum would come out in her dressing gown, her face shiny with cream and her hair in rollers. A nice boy, she'd tell everyone, and I'd say Mum, he's dull as dishwater. I had to end up marrying someone dangerous.

"She's always going on about how handsome Toby is. It's like she puts him on display. D'you think he is?"

"In spite of the hairy ears? Yes."

"Maybe I will be when I'm his age, then."

"You are already."

"No, I'm not. I'm young, that's different. You'll just have to wait and see."

Don't say that, Tom.

∞

She's only half-awake when he asks, "Aly? How about what he called me?"

"Unfair. You're not little and you're certainly no twerp, Tom," she replies drowsily.

She hears his laughter in the darkness, and she starts to laugh, too. With a single swift motion, he lifts her on top of him, and she's thrust, still laughing, into wakefulness. Her head's pulled back hard by the hair, and she only exults at the gusto of Tom's attack, at the exuberance of the search conducted by his mouth from ear-lobe to breast, at that instinct of her own that gives her the power of wild movement upon him long past the point that should be exhaustion, until the moment when their laughter stops. She falls onto his heaving chest, inert, his hands still tangled in her hair and his kisses, gentle now in victory, on the eyelids she lacks the strength to lift.

The alarm startles her eyes open. Monday. School, as if nothing has changed. She sinks back on the pillow next to Tom, who hasn't stirred. This morning, once more, I can look at him. And tomorrow morning too. Until . . . I don't know when.

And then she thinks: I've never in my life before done it laughing. I never knew you could.

CHAPTER SIX

He goes to school calmly, and calmly works in the small
room where he's pinned up above what has become his desk an
airline poster of the Colosseum, a picture cut out of a magazine
of a Harley-Davidson, and some cartoons that don't seem to her
particularly funny. They're mostly about computers, however,
so she wouldn't know. Sometimes he sits up very late, working,
much later than she can when she's got to get up early. Then
when he slips naked into bed beside her, having dropped his
jeans and T-shirt in a heap by the side of the bed, where they'll
remain until she decides to do something about them, or he
needs them again, whichever is the sooner, he often whispers,
"Aly?" or he simply starts to make love to her, rousing her out of
one kind of unconsciousness, drawing her down into another. It
makes no discernible difference to him in the morning, though

it does to her. If he crashes in the afternoon, he sleeps so heavily that nothing can wake him. Like a kid.

His lute lessons continue as before. Nothing is said, so they're being paid for. He's not being cut off, not from his education, and he in turn is faithful. Most days he practises. "You did say you wanted to hear. It's not too boring, is it?" It isn't. Even the repetition of phrases over and over is beautiful to her. It accompanies her life. Sometimes she sits, pretending to read, and watches him: his intent expression, his hands.

Or she cooks. One evening, standing at the kitchen counter, slitting pods to reveal broad beans nestled in soft white hollows, she hears him singing. She doesn't know the song, she doesn't know any of the things he plays. *Amarilli mia bella . . .* That's easy: Amaryllis, she'd be a nymph or a shepherdess, something like that? *Amarilli e 'l mio amore . . .* He's just learning it, because he stops in a couple of places and begins again, or tries something different. *O del mio cor dolce desio . . .* oh, sweet desire of my heart, my heart's delight. His voice is these days a tenor, with an untrained huskiness in it. This song is the loveliest thing she's ever heard. She puts down the knife and tries to stem the tears with a paper towel.

After a while he simply stops, comes into the kitchen, and asks if she wants any chopping done. He doesn't seem to notice the signs of weeping, or perhaps he just thinks it's onions.

She said to him at the beginning, I'm not a very good cook.

And he said, that's OK, I am. Neither of these things is strictly true. She's her mother's kind of plain cook, and he's picked up a few of Louise's simpler recipes and some of her tricks. His pasta, like Louise's, is always al dente. She knows now why Louise so often made pasta. It's because he eats so much. Whereas she used to come home from work and have an egg on toast, he's always ravenous. Music may be the food of love, she thinks, sniffing away the last of the tears, but food is the food of love, too.

She also goes to school, but not so calmly. There's been an outbreak of vandalism. It started with graffiti, and splotches of paint on walls. Then small fires during the night.

The official word is that it's an invasion of elements from the great pool of disturbed individuals Outside, but it's pupils, of course, sneaking in somehow, doing these things. "Demonstrating their appreciation of us the only way they know how," says someone in the staff room, and they all laugh. It is revenge. For what? For some forgotten slight? Or for something quite other, some disaster or violence in one of the pleasant homes along the lawn-lined streets around the school?

And yet, she can't help being protective. When Tom says, "You know, the girls at your school've got a bit of a reputation," she replies, "Do you mind not talking like that? It's very sexist," at which he colours and mumbles, "Sorry." He speaks little of his school, a very different kind of place, with its chapel, and its choir, and its hordes of gardeners. Occasionally he volunteers a general comment, such as that teachers ought not to discuss pop music, or at least they ought to stick to the Beatles and things they know about, because if they try to keep up they're always two groups behind and make themselves ridiculous, but otherwise she hears little of them either. When one day he recounts a story involving the trashing of someone's house—bathrooms, exercise room, grand piano and all—at a party while the parents were away, and the subsequent search for the culprits, she's actually quite pleased. So all is not sweetness and light in the bastion of privilege for which Toby and Louise are still paying.

His standard of living has taken a nose-dive. Instead of the leafy vistas of home, there's only her small balcony. The flat was advertised with "harbour glimpses," which means that if you crane your neck from the end of the balcony, you can see a sliver of blue almost blotted out by a gas storage tank. But the lorikeets come down to the balcony, and there are some who know him already. Clinging to the edges of her hanging baskets, brighter than the flowers, they bob their heads and utter squeaks of impatience until he comes out with a handful of seeds. For his own needs, petrol for the bike and computer magazines mostly, he seems to have a bit left of his savings. Whatever it was that this was originally intended for, he doesn't say. From the library he gets piles of thick books on buildings, bridges, cities.

She has her homework, too. One evening, she's marking test papers and he happens to be standing behind her eating one of the snacks that he requires at intervals after his dinner's gone down. He spreads peanut butter more thickly than she would have thought possible, and as often as not leaves the gloppy knife just as it is on the counter. If she mentions it, he obligingly cleans up, just as he's happy enough to help her wash and dry dishes when called upon, but he's already past the stage where he might have learned to notice any necessity for it by himself. One thing he does think of doing is iron shirts. He seems to be quite particular about that. But then he'll just leave the iron and walk away. Certainly Louise meant to bring up a son who understood housework, she often said so, but she must have been too busy, and the fact that a Vietnamese couple come in to clean the house by the harbour every week hasn't helped.

He glances over her shoulder. "Oh, Tiffany," he says. Alyson looks down at the name, decorated with scrolls, with daisies for dots. No effort has been spared on T, ff and y, but much has been spared on the actual answers to the questions.

"You know her?"

"She's a friend of mine." Is that a note of caution?

"A pretty girl." Why did I say that?

"She's not short of a boyfriend. Can I see?"

"No. Go away."

Jealous of Tiffany? She looks again at the paper, finds a few things marked wrong that could conceivably be considered half-right, bumps the score up a few points just to be on the safe side.

This too had to happen.

She's been living in hope of making it to the end of the year with her secret inviolate, at least at school, not looking any further ahead than that. It would be foolish to believe that it could be anything other than just a matter of time. But please, let these weeks pass in peace.

After the last class of the morning, Tiffany appears out of nowhere, standing in her path. "Look," she says.

What is the girl doing? She's reaching into the neck of her uniform blouse. Slowly, so as not to break it, she draws a gold chain from under the Peter Pan collar. She holds out delicately between finger and thumb her name, written in gold, complete with an underline scroll.

"Like it? It's a birthday present from Mum."

"It's lovely." Alyson touches a fingertip beneath the loop of the y.

"I suppose you think it's a silly name."

"No, I don't. Why should I think that?"

"Because you think I'm called after some stupid upmarket shop in a city my mother's never been to. But it's not that. It's an old name. Look it up. Or ask him. *He* found it in a book."

Alyson feels her eyelids fly wide open. She's looking straight into Tiffany's eyes, which are a bright, clear blue. She draws back. Groups of kids, just released from class, go around them on the path. A voice chirps, "Listen! Listen to this!" Tiffany's eyes hold hers, unwavering.

And then Tiffany's face changes. The challenge in it fades, and what is left is grief.

I have won, thinks Alyson. But what were the rules?

Carefully, Tiffany drops the chain back into the neck of her blouse, and walks away.

Just as carefully, Alyson makes her way towards the staff room. She is not exactly trembling; her whole body is vibrating. And when she sits down at her desk, she feels, as her mother would say, like a wet rag.

Her first thought is: soon they'll all know. There's nothing I can do to stop it.

And then she thinks: I was very short of a boyfriend.

Behind her, everything is as usual. How's this? The cat knocked a bottle of oyster sauce over my homework and walked in it. Good one. She's got them all believing her auntie the midwife delivered a baby with a human body and a sheep's head and now it's being brought up in a secret orphanage for monsters. Mel, that girl's old enough to use deodorant, the other kids are holding their noses.

"I'll have a word with her," says Mel resignedly. Then, "OK, you sophisticates, how about my place Friday night? I'm warning you now, we won't be talking about anything but cricket and cats. And I don't mean T. S. Eliot. *No* culture. Bring beer, bring plonk. No boutique wines, please. Alyson? Alyson, are you all right?"

It isn't until that night, when she's sitting on the balcony in the warm night air, listening to him practise inside, that she thinks: he hurt her. He exploited her, and it was because of me. He might not have known how much she wanted him. But he's a boy, and he might have done it anyway. How should I know?

"Tom," she asks. "Why me?"

He raises himself on one elbow from the pillow, and looks down at her. "Why? Why are you asking me?"

"I just want to know."

He gently pinches her nipple, kisses it, takes it between his teeth and flicks it with his tongue. She suppresses the sound that rises to her lips. When he's satisfied with what he's done, he moves on. "There's one reason," he says, in his own good time. "They're like rosebuds."

"Tom."

"That's another one, the way you say my name. The first time
you really said it, you said 'Thank you, Tom.' Remember? And it
was like I'd never heard it before. I love your voice, Aly."

Her fingers follow his eyebrow, his cheekbone. "No. You
know what I'm asking. About how unusual this is. That you—"
She falters. His face has clouded over. "We've never talked about
it," she finishes weakly.

"Is that what you're thinking about? When we're like this? It's
unusual?"

"No! I didn't mean—"

"Then, why should I?" He swallows hard.

She begins to speak, but he sees she's going to take back
the question, puts his hand quickly over her mouth. "No, you
asked. All right, Aly, listen. *Da capo.* I remember more about
you than you think, from a long time ago. You mightn't want
to hear about it, but to me it's good, everything. After that, I
couldn't talk to you to save my life, for . . . it must have been
for years. But I used to hang around when you were there.
Sneaking looks around corners. You liked me when I was little, but you weren't interested in me when I got bigger. You
never noticed I still liked you, did you?"

"No, I never did."

"Just as well. Look, I'm not saying when I got older I would have come after you. I wouldn't have thought it was possible. I'm not saying I wasn't interested in other girls."

"I'm not a girl, Tom! That's what I mean!"

"Don't mess me around with words, Aly. You're going to make me upset. If I said other women, that'd be wrong too. You asked me, I'm trying to explain. Are you going to let me, or not?"

No words.

He takes a deep breath. "The way it was—I never had to ask what most people have to ask. What the songs are about. Is this the one for me, is this what I really want, all that. I couldn't believe—even now, I can hardly believe it—there you were, just sitting in the train. I felt so lucky! It was all new, and yet it wasn't. I looked at you, and you were beautiful. And you looked at me—" He reddens. "Like you were interested."

She gasps, raises her head in protest, but he presses her down. "Don't pretend, Aly. You asked! You already told me, the day I first kissed you—I remember every word you said—you told me you knew those Fridays on the train meant something. Now I'm telling you, I knew from the beginning." Her blush must be as deep as his. After all the things that've been done and said between them, here they are in bed blushing at each other.

"Then you knew too much."

"I was looking for it. You weren't. You would have thought it was

wrong. You did think it was wrong. That's why I had to go first."
He throws himself back on the pillow, looks up at the ceiling. "I
know that doesn't really answer why. But if you ask me, that's all I
can say. I could ask you. Why are you here now with me, and not
someone else? Someone older, that could take you places further
than the mountains? I could ask you that. Don't ask me anything
else, Aly. Don't. It'll never sound like it makes sense, it just is."

It just is.

No salsa at Mel's. It's sausages and tomato sauce and white
bread, beer and plonk, as promised, in the backyard. Mel and
Annie are renovating the house, working from the back. The
front rooms are a clutter of ladders, dust-sheets, paint-pots drip-
ping onto old newspapers, and a rented sanding machine.
Alyson has filed in to one of them with a group of murmuring
sightseers, but as they file out after Annie, on the way to admir-
ing a floor stripped back to the original boards, Mel's hand
clamps around her wrist.

"Just a moment, Alyson." She shuts the door. "What's this I
hear?"

"What do you hear?"

"I hear you're living with a Year Eleven."

"No. Yes." But this is no way to speak of him. "He's a person,
Mel."

"A person."

"Not one of ours."

"I know that."

"So you know all you need to know."

"No, I don't. I don't know what I'm going to say if I get asked."

"Say it's nobody's business but mine."

"I don't think that's going to do you a lot of good." Mel's clear, scrubbed face is set hard. "I never would have thought this of you."

"He's almost seventeen."

"Alyson, for God's sake! It's not as if I've never heard of it before, but you! I thought you would have had more common sense. More discretion."

"That's funny, so did I."

"Then we've both been wrong."

"Does everybody know?"

"They will soon." Mel opens the door. "They won't hear it from me," she says. "But I'm disappointed in you, Alyson." She picks up a cat that comes slinking round her ankles. "You should have taken a kitten when I offered."

The kid who stabs another kid, not fatally, not even seriously, at the back of the canteen, has come to school with her brother's wicked hunting knife and a bag packed ready for running away. The bag contains all the necessities of life: a couple of unidentified pills twisted in plastic wrap, cigarettes, a packet of condoms, and a bikini (bottom only). Alyson is on duty, but she's covered. She's there, when and where she's was supposed to be, she's standing staring into space at the time in full view of the canteen helpers. She just doesn't happen to see.

"You haven't got eyes in the back of your head," says the policewoman, getting into the car. "Little buggers."

The kids are back in class, and Bill is watching Alyson's. The Boss turns towards the Office. Parents. Reports. "You're covered," he says.

"Lucky," remarks Mel.

Luckier than I deserve.

A few days later, in a free period, she's studying the syllabus, thinking about next year's set books. Contemporary English Course. Contemporary Issues (i) Cultural Identity. Mudrooroo, *Wild Cat Falling*. The phone rings in the next room. Someone will get it. She chews her pencil. Tom says she shouldn't. It's bad for your teeth, he says. He really thinks he knows everything General Course (iv) Topic Area Elective (b) Crossing Boundaries. There's Nadine Gordimer. Good.

"Alyson, the Boss wants to see you."

She tucks in her blouse, puts on her jacket. You always think these things will help when your luck's run out.

∞

The school secretary's jacket has shoulders padded just about up to her ears, and her glasses shine. "He said go in. He's on the phone."

Alyson knocks, goes in, receives a nod, sits down. He's talking to a parent. A case of shoplifting, by the sound of it. Removal to grandparents' home in some very distant location an option he supports. He doesn't look well. He has had all these problems recently. She clasps her damp hands on her knee, unclasps them. A giveaway. She can't look at him while he's on the phone, so she stares at the picture above his chair. A desert, a hint of trees. Red sky. She seems to have seen this picture in every Principal's office she's been in for the last ten years or so. Is this a peculiarity of taste, or is there a central warehouse that supplies these things? When she started teaching, it was minor Impressionists. Streaky streets in Paris. From her own schooldays, a memory surfaces of a vaguely Oriental woman with a green face. And the Queen. Now the Queen's fading, the woman with the green face is no more, even the Impressionists aren't what they used to be. But the desert's still here. The Boss leans back in his chair, fiddles with a pen as he talks. Like a male gynaecologist, he keeps a photo, intended to instil confidence, on the desk. His wife and children, with narrow snouts and tiny round eyes, look like a family of ferrets.

The Boss puts down the phone. "I think you know what this is about, Alyson."

"I'm not sure I do."

"Alyson. I have had several phone calls within the last forty-eight hours, concerning your . . . your personal situation. One from Mrs. Gabrielli—Professor Gabrielli."

Not only gossip, then. It's Louise. "Professor McCarthy."

"Oh, right. Yes. I stand corrected. The other one from the Principal of the other school, er, involved."

"Involved?"

"Of course, they're involved, Alyson. They have a pastoral responsibility. The phone call, however, was on a personal basis only."

"Just man to man."

"Don't dig your heels in with me, Alyson. No-one wants to make more of a fuss than necessary. Possibly a momentary . . . lamentable, yes . . . an episode. Far be it from me. A blip, if you will, on an otherwise—" He taps an irritable finger. "I'm telling you, we do not need this."

"It's my own life." This is abysmal.

"Is it? The parents don't share your view of the matter. Nor is it my view, Alyson. What kind of example is this? And from you. I've always considered you one of the best teachers I've ever had." Ah. Familiar ground. His ground, Mel's, her own. I never would have thought this of you. I'm disappointed in you. What would your parents think if they knew? "Now. Cast your memory back to the incident of Monday last."

"I'm covered!"

"Yes, and so it's been reported. But just between you and me, the mind's not on the job, is it? It could have been a child's life. And who knows what would have come out, in the . . . the subsequent publicity, and then where would we be?"

There's nothing to say to this.

"As it is, if and when it becomes common knowledge, it won't make anything easier for anybody, Alyson, least of all yourself. You may consider that your predilections are your own affair, but in this case—"

She starts out of the chair.

"—I suggest to you that you consider your position. Try to come to some understanding with the parents." He pauses. "Seek help, perhaps?"

"Help?"

"Up to you, Alyson. Up to you. We're coming to the end of the year, thank the Lord, and I want you to come back next year—I don't think there's a transfer for you in the offing—with all this sorted out. That's all. Get it sorted out."

There's nowhere to go, nowhere to get away and think. But what is there to think about? She must just go back to her desk, and sit and wait for whatever else will come, in the way of sidelong glances in the staff room and smothered giggles in class, not knowing whether they really have anything to do with her or whether she's imagining them; and for the holidays, and the chance to pretend for a while that none of this is happening.

She thinks of those Friday afternoons in her bedroom. How they could have stayed there a little bit longer, how that was all she needed.

This is what it's like out in the world.

She can't tell him of her humiliation, she doesn't mention "predilection." She does tell him that his mother has called, and his school.

"What can they do to you?"

"Depends how hard they're leaned on."

"But this is a matter of human rights," he says earnestly.

She has to smile. "I don't see myself making a big case out of it, Tom. 'Teacher Defends Right to Love.' I don't think so."

"I don't, either, when you put it like that." He looks at her steadily. "You just said 'love.'"

"So I did."

He takes her hand. "I'm encouraged. Not too much, though. No harm done."

"Tom, has anyone said anything to you?"

"A few of the kids. Nothing really."

"What have they said?"

"You don't want to hear. But they don't know what to make of it, Aly. I don't think they actually believe it. Not a problem."

"They've dropped you."

"I had to be dropped. I'm not at home, I don't give anyone this phone number, and I don't do things with them any more. It doesn't matter." She is ashamed. He's self-contained, as Louise said, and more than that, he has spared her. She hasn't let herself think that so soon he might have lost his friends. But that reserve is also his protection. He's not needy, therefore not vulnerable, they've known him long enough to understand that. He's cut himself off, and it's on his own terms. He goes on quickly, so she can't ask more. "But I'd better try and talk to Toby and Louise, Aly. I'll go over at Christmas. Until then, let's forget it."

Exactly what she wants to do.

On the first Saturday morning of the holidays, they're out shopping. He's led her to the edge of the pavement to show her how a pair of mynah birds are stealing blueberries and stashing them behind the wheel of a parked car. One runs across to the blueberry box, just out of the line of sight of the greengrocer, snatches a berry, runs back with it. Then the other sets out.

"Alyson!"

She jumps, and her smile wavers, reappears differently.

"Bill."

"Enjoying your holidays?"

"Yes. Hello, Christine." Bill stands foursquare, eyebrows raised in a friendly manner. He's not going away. "This is Tom."

Tom, unsmiling, nods. Anything more would have been a miscalculation.

"Your nephew?"

"No."

"Oh, sorry." He looks very unsorry indeed.

They stand in silence. I'll stand here forever, she thinks. If that's what it takes.

Bill will have crowed at home, guess what! His wife surely knows, and it's she who cracks. "So many presents to buy, so little time! Happy Christmas, Alyson."

"You too."

They stay for a while where they are.

"Fourteen berries," says Tom, taking the shopping bag. "They're good together, aren't they?"

They drive almost every day to a quiet beach. It's not really swimmable, that's why it's quiet. The waves are too high, you can see the sandbanks shifting. There's no lifeguard, no shop. They mess around in the shallows.

Tom takes a series of rockpool pictures, and some of her, topless. Why not, now? And after all, it makes him happy. He's said, let your hair grow a bit, and she has. He was right. The kink that used to be her despair in damp weather now falls in untidier but more fashionable ringlets. He likes to twist the strands around his fingers. When she sees the photos, she thinks, now my hair looks retro, too. And the wide straw hat. Maybe I look like his great-grandmother, or mine. She fancies this idea, a blurring of the eras.

He gives no sign of being bored by the way they spend these days, but she can't help wondering: "Isn't this all too quiet for you?"

"You mean I should be out raging?"

"I suppose so."

"You know what that's for, Aly. It's hoping there'll be some of this at the end of it." He slides a hand under her as she lies face-down on the sandy beach-towel. "Who needs it?"

Another thing she hasn't thought of. Not for him the anxieties of who goes home with whom from the disco, preoccupation with low-level esoterica, bra-straps and such, mothers with creamy faces. He's skipped a whole phase, and in spite of everything he's pretty pleased with himself.

CHAPTER SEVEN

She's got a small Christmas tree for the mantelpiece, and he arranges the ballerina and the red devil on top of it. They're holding on to each other and waving, as if to a crowd.

He's assembled presents for his family. Soap with herbs roughly embedded in it for Toby. Glass ball earrings, like Christmas decorations, bought off a street stall for Griselda. He's framed a drawing of his own, a village scene from the Italian holiday, for Louise, and another for his grandmother. He's asked her several times what she thinks about these things. "They're perfect," she says. Watching him wrap them on Christmas Eve, fiddling with paper and ribbon, tying a knot and then undoing it, she feels for him a sense of apprehension that in the daytime the sunlight sparkling off the water has kept at bay.

Christmas morning is sunny, and she wakes to find him enthusiastically making love to her.

"I know you wanted it to stay the way we were before. I know what's happened is my fault," he says. "But Aly, if it hadn't happened, we wouldn't have this morning!"

She's found a book for him on the history of urban planning. It looks very dry to her, with a lot of diagrams, but not unlike the sort of thing he pores over from the library. He falls on it with joy, and spread-eagled on the bed starts turning the pages. She puts on the CD he's given her, and music rises into the room. It's something new to her, the songs of a woman who composed, in seventeenth-century Venice, the kind of music he plays. He's thought about this. He wants to find a way to teach her. "I know you'll like it! She was really brilliant, Barbara Strozzi!" he burst out even before she'd got it unwrapped. "She wrote madrigals, cantatas—here's one, *'Lagrime mie,'* my tears— Look, this is her!" There's a portrait of the composer, lace bodice slipping from a bare breast, with flowers in her hair, holding not a lute like his, but a viol, he's explained. Now he breaks off from his reading, takes her hand. "Listen!" he says. *"Si, si, pensiero* . . . Yes, yes, let me think. . . . *una canzon troviamo* . . . See, the singer, he's a shepherd—you know how they are— he's trying to find the right love song, he's flipping through his music, but his mood's changing all the time. She parodies all the different styles—she's great!" He looks at her expectantly. She thinks of the men she's known whose feet have begun to hurt the minute they got into a gallery, who've taken her to concerts and then been indulgent, at best, when she came out high.

"It's lovely!" she says. She doesn't understand it yet, but it is.

"You really like it?"

"I love it. I love you, Tom."

And now he forgets even the music, but it's there filling all the sunlit air around them. "Aly, say it, say it! I want to hear you say it over and over!" She does, she says it over and over, almost often enough. It's long been far, far too late not to encourage him.

There's nothing slow about her mother. The telephone is no barrier. "You're not spending the day alone, are you, darling?"

"No, Mum."

"Is this the same one you were so worried about last Christmas?"

"Yes, Mum."

"He isn't married." Not if he's with you on Christmas Day, she means.

"No, Mum."

"I have been a bit concerned. That's never a good idea, my love."

She knows there's something, she knows there are a lot of other ideas that aren't good ones. But she's not going to think of this. Not even Mum.

When she hangs up, he says, "I have to go over there, Aly."

She is alone for most of the afternoon. The time passes slowly. But if he's away so long, perhaps it's going well. Fidgety, she leaves a note, goes out for a walk. There's nobody on the street, but in the park by the water she sees a child on a new tricycle, another with a remote-control model car that won't work on the grass, sated parents lying silently under trees, and the couple who live across the hall, just walking, too. A balding, stout, young middle-aged man, a not-pretty girl. She's seen their flat through the open door sometimes. Very little furniture. No-one comes to see them, either. She looks at them with sympathy, but sees no sign in their indifferent greeting that they reciprocate. They must have an opinion of her situation with Tom, as she has of theirs. Or perhaps not.

When she gets back, their door is open. "Did you see anyone coming out the back way?" the man shouts to her.

"What? No."

"We've been burgled! Someone's climbed up the outside—in the window, out this door! With the TV, my computer, everything!"

"My rings!" cries the girl. "They had sentimental value, that's all! Who could do something like this on Christmas Day?"

"Druggies!" he yells at her, "You think everybody's Christians? Who left the window open? We're not insured!" It's just occurred to him.

"I'm sorry," says Alyson. They wouldn't be insured, would they? She goes into her own place, looks around. Nothing is disturbed. There's Tom's book, open on the bed. She hears cars, voices, but she doesn't go out, and nobody comes to ask her again if she saw anything.

She waits.

When he comes home, he's very quiet.

She sits beside him on the sofa. After a while he says, "It's no use."

"I should have talked to them."

"Wouldn't have done any good."

He takes a card from his shirt pocket. It's one of the miniature, almost plain white Christmas cards favoured by Louise. There's an embossed Christmas tree with a single red spot for the star on top. Inside it is a cheque for seventy-five dollars, signed by Toby. The message on the card says: To Tom, our son. Love from Dad (Toby) and Mum (Louise).

Would he have forgotten who they were?

"They said they hardly know me."

"That must be how they—"

"It's a territorial dispute," he says. "They don't care how I feel."

"What's this?"

"That's from Griselda." It's a pencil case shaped like a guitar. "And from Maura." His grandmother has given him an expensive fountain pen.

The telephone rings. "Don't answer it," he says urgently.

She answers it. "Are you satisfied, Alyson?" screams Louise. "This is the worst Christmas of my life. You sent my son to me full of hostility! You've done a wonderful job. You've brainwashed him. He was a loving, loving boy, before you got your claws into him! I can't believe you were once my friend, I never would have believed you could betray me like this! You disgust me! Now what is it you want? Tell me! What more do you want?"

Tom grabs the phone. "Stop this," he says. Then he puts it down.

Her hand has gone automatically to her forehead, as if she's been hit.

She manages to say, "It's Christmas. There's a lot of emotion."

"And a lot to drink," he says. "We'll go out." He goes into the kitchen, pulls down her shopping basket. He puts in it the Christmas cake her mother's sent, a piece of ham, cheese, bread. A bottle of wine. A knife, glasses. "Get your keys, Aly."

So they spend the night on the beach. He eats a lot of what

they've brought. Nothing seems to spoil his appetite. Then, he pushes everything aside onto the sand, lifts the blanket over the two of them.

She raises herself up, looks nervously around. It's very dark now. The lights from the parking area don't reach them. The tide's coming in, but she can hardly see the white of the waves that sound so close.

He pulls her down. "Have you ever done this before?"

"No."

"Me either. It's the first time for both of us."

It's very different from the morning. Night and day.

The waves are coming very close by the time she's aware of them again

She lifts her skirt, walks into the shocking, blessed coldness of the foaming water.

"Be careful, Aly. Give me your hand."

Nothing in her life now bears any resemblance to what it was before. No wonder they don't know him. She doesn't know herself.

It's getting light again by the time she follows him up the stairs, trailing her damp skirt.

He puts the phone under a heap of cushions and shuts the door on it, and they go to bed and sleep through most of the next day.

On New Year's Eve they hear from the balcony the ships' horns calling to each other up and down the harbour at midnight. People who are at parties screaming "Happy New Year!" never hear this, and there have been times when she's been alone on this night and been afraid to hear it. Even now, the thought of the dark water slapping the ships' sides and of the moon-streaked ocean waiting for them beyond the Heads makes her press her lips into Tom's warm neck, wrap her arms around him.

"I'll be seventeen soon," he says with satisfaction.

She hears her mother say, "Don't wish away the years." She can't do that now, even for him.

In the morning, she feels terrible. She has to pee all the time and it's very painful. It gets worse. "I think I have to go to the doctor," she says. There must be some clinic open on New Year's Day. Panicky, he looks for one in the phone book. She tries not to let him see her face screwed up, not to scare him more. She tries not to writhe.

"You stay here," she says.

"I'll come with you. I can drive."

"You can't."

"In an emergency. I can take care of you, Aly."

The doctor is elderly. Pink, jowly, kind. "It's what they call a honeymoon problem," he says. Her face burns. Antibiotics for the infection, drink lots of water, no intercourse till it clears up. "Find something else to pass the time," he adds jovially. Courteously, he heaves himself to his feet, escorts her to the door. When he sees Tom, obviously waiting for her, obviously not a son, he doesn't turn a hair. "Happy New Year," is all he says. For this alone, she could kiss him, if she didn't feel so awful.

"You are good, Tom," she says. He's tucked her up, put pills and water by the bed. He might be feeling contrite, though that's the last thing she wants, but it's not the first time he's been good in this way. Soon after he came to stay, she had a bad period. Well, he was quite good. At first she was shy, not wanting to gross out one so young, but he thought it was funny that what she took for it was Cointreau, and had a glass with her, and then he got amorous. It's a turn-on, he said. There's not a lot that isn't a turn-on. That's her problem now. It's to Louise's credit, this is one way of looking at it, that she's raised a son who's not afraid of women. Or even of Louise herself, in spite of how she's acting. I'm more scared of her than he is, she thinks. If she's thinking about me this minute, and she could be, I wonder if she's giving me any credit at all? No. I can't hope that she is.

When she's feeling better, but still a bit fragile, Griselda turns up. "I'm here secretly," she proclaims. "They'd kill me."

"They wouldn't kill you," he says.

She tosses her head. "Aly, you know my mother's a cow!"

"Don't think Aly wants to get involved in your adolescent power struggles," he says scornfully. "If she said anything, you'd be just as likely to quote her. That'd help a lot."

"I wouldn't! I'm not entirely unsympathetic to your point of view."

"Big deal," he says.

"I miss you, Tom. I miss your dopey music. Aren't you coming home? I know Christmas Day was a write-off, they're very stressed out, and they got stuck into the champagne in the morning, but they really want you home."

"No."

"Then can I stay tonight?"

"No, you can't stay!" they say at the same time, and this makes them laugh.

"Don't laugh without me!" cries Griselda.

They drive her home, but drop her at the end of the street and watch her the rest of the way. "It isn't a lot of fun for her," he says.

He goes to the pool and swims a number of lengths that she finds incredible. Then he dozes with his head in her lap while she watches a programme on Jane Austen. He hardly ever reads novels, it turns out, unless they're on the list. Even then, it seems he believes that any exam question can be answered based on a cursory reading, using a certain theory of his own. It's not exactly the first time she's heard this one, but the irritating thing is that he's a very fast reader, and according to what he tells her of his marks, it more or less works for him. "Wouldn't it be easier to just read it properly?" she asked. Apparently it's a matter of principle. It was Louise's son she was ashamed to show her thriller to on the train, not Tom. "Probably it was the tutorials at the dinner table," he said. 'What do you think it means, Tom, lighting out for the territory? Do you think Huckleberry was a racist?' She was only trying to get me going. It works with some things, but it doesn't work with stories." He likes movies that started out as movies. *Casablanca. The Seven Samurai,* and all the Hollywood and spaghetti spin-offs. Very new or very old movies are best, she thinks, so they don't get caught up in things that she remembers and he doesn't. When there's a movie with more blood in it than she can take, it's her turn to lie in his arms and seem to sleep. She can read murder mysteries, but she can't watch. Violence on the screen distresses him not at all. He's never known it.

There are things she used to like to do while she watched TV that she doesn't now. She doesn't do exercises to flatten her stomach, or even yoga. She doesn't knit, though there was a cotton short-sleeved sweater she meant to make this summer. He mightn't think anything of it, but she doesn't want to take the risk that one night he'll look at her and be reminded of someone middle-aged. What an idiot.

But Tom has his own areas of sensitivity. One morning, he's in the kitchen. She hears him rummaging around for something sufficiently substantial to keep him going till lunch, against a background of radio voices. He hums along with a jingle. Then after a while the chatter, at once so idle and so effortful, turns to the subject of an actress and her toy boy. A cupboard door closes, there's Tom's light footstep, and it's switched off, abruptly, mid-chuckle.

Her heart gives a little twist. Don't worry, Tom. You're not old enough.

When Louise rings again, he's at the library. This time it seems Louise is trying to be calm, but she asks the same question: what is it you want?

How to answer? "What is it you want, Louise?"

"Send my son home."

"I can't send him."

"Are you saying you would if you could?"

Does she really want to know? This I can answer. "No, I'm not saying that."

"Then I've got nothing to say to you. You're *vile!*"

Vile.

She doesn't tell him about this one.

Bushfires have broken out in the mountains. To the west there's a red glow on the horizon, day and night. Black leaves spin slowly down, settling in the city streets, the day she goes to meet Katie at the Library coffee shop.

"You had to pick your friend's son," says Katie. "And not only your friend, but *Louise.*"

"I didn't pick him."

"You mean . . . oh. Well. I understand that sometimes a kid might get something like this into his head, but it's an adult's responsibility—"

"If he were not by now—in this respect, at least—an adult, too." Her hands are clasped hard on the edge of the table in front of her. How many times do I have to have this interview?

"It's a taboo, Aly! There are reasons for it."

"I can't help that." This is being more defiant than she feels.

"A teacher—"

"I am *not* HIS teacher." It's difficult to shout softly.

"Don't get upset, Aly. Two cappuccinos, please. You have to admit this is something—"

"I admit that. I admit everything."

"And what's in it for you. Aly?" Katie leans forward, lowers her voice further. "Isn't it just sex? What do you talk about?"

"That is not a problem."

"You've regressed to the intellectual level of a sixteen-year-old?"

"It must be all those years of teaching."

"Please, Aly. Remember who this is. Haven't we known each other long enough? If a friend— Look. Eric. Now can it be . . . that you're attracted to a young boy because he's unthreatening?" Katie sits back. An insight! "Just think about it."

"I don't have to think about it. When you've been threatened, unthreatening means something. It does not explain Tom. Spare me the analysis, Katie." As she speaks, though, she thinks: Katie looks worn and unhappy. "Next thing you'll be telling me he wants a mother. Well, he's got a mother. And by the way, was this Louise's idea?"

"I understand how she feels."

"So do I."

"You're not a mother."

"Neither are you."

Katie bursts into tears.

"Oh, Aly, did you know I was still trying?" Alyson shakes her head helplessly. Katie gasps the words out from behind a hand held over her mouth, as if hoping to keep them in. "The treatment! They say a little discomfort, but it's so painful. The pills make you see double. And every time you go back, the doctor's receptionist is so appallingly smiley! She knows all about you, and she says things like 'Oh, bad luck,' or 'Better luck next time!' She means well, I mean well. Aly, I'm sorry!"

"Katie—" Poor Katie. Imagine putting yourself through so much pain just so you can have a bored little Brian.

"That's not really it!" sobs Katie. "While I'm going through all this! Brian! He kept talking about people who have sex with students, and students who put notes under people's office doors. And I suddenly thought, he's doing it. And how did I know? Because I put notes under his door when I was his student, Aly!"

"You *did?*" Such a studious girl she was then, Katie. Good God.

"You couldn't imagine the notes I put— Thank you," she says politely, looking away from the waiter, who can see perfectly well what's going on.

"Katie, you might be wrong." But false comfort is no comfort. And Tom wouldn't suppose for a moment that she's wrong.

"I'm not wrong." The hand comes away from her mouth. "A student threatened him for harassment. For a while, and then it went away, it never came to anything. He said it was nothing, but I knew it was something. I was not wrong."

"What are you going to do?"

"I don't know. I'm not sure I can forgive his stupidity, apart from anything else. I have to think." She wipes her nose. "So now you know. I feel better. I'm sorry I was so censorious. I do know you, Aly. You might be a bit . . . carried away, but I don't think you'd do it lightly. You know Louise. Everybody . . . of course, everyone's embarrassed, and horribly curious, including me, but the consensus is, you're off your nut." She smiles blearily. "Got a tissue? Thanks. Not for being *tempted* to pinch Tom away from her, or even for taking him up on it or whatever the story is, surprising though it may be. He's lovely, that's a given, the hair, the eyes, the lute and everything. People have been saying for years, he's going to be a more impressive specimen than Toby, even—"

They have? And I never thought about him at all! The lute? Yes, the lute is sexy. Probably not what Louise meant by it.

"—and with any luck not such a big head on him. Not for any of that, but for actually getting in the ring with Louise," finishes Katie.

"I'm so glad to be providing a bit of sport."

"Well, people . . . I've even heard it said—by someone that hardly knows you, mind you, this was at a party—it's because you're a bit childlike yourself. The gentle manner, though *I* know that can be deceptive, the plumpness, beg your pardon, Aly, *slight* plumpness, the crinkly hair, the skirts . . ."

"If that's the best they can do, I think I've heard enough," says Alyson, stonily now.

Katie licks chocolate-dusted froth off her spoon. "The thing is, what are you going to do?"

"I don't know."

"Why don't you just . . . let him go home. And wait till he's a little bit older."

"Let him." Let him. Send him.

"I don't mean let him, no, I don't really mean that. I mean, just wait. Till he's twenty, say?"

Twenty. There's a poem. *What is love? I remember, 'tis not hereafter . . . Then come kiss me, sweet and twenty . . .* "That's a long time." By then, who knows? She tries to smile. "I'd be exactly twice his age."

"Better than now. And you'd only be twice his age once. After that it's downhill all the way," points out Katie. "I'd better get back. Oh, Alyson. I don't know whether to feel sorry for you— or what."

It's cooler at home. You can't see the red glare from here. There's a note under the devil. *Gone to pool.* An emphatic *T* inside a heart.

What is love? Isn't there another answer? A setting of it for voice and lute was on a CD Tom borrowed from his lute teacher. Now what is love I pray thee tell, It is that fountain and that well Where pleasures and repentance dwell. Something something. It is a sunshine mix'd with rain, It is a gentle pleasing pain, A flower that dies and springs again. Yes, all right. Let that one go.

She turns on the TV. Daytime TV, now this is something that's almost never a good idea. One of those tabloid talk shows. Women who fantasize about a pop singer she's never heard of while making love with their husbands. A husband whines, "I empathize with her." The singer's face projected behind them, simpering. Alyson takes off her bra, rubs the red mark it's left. It's the hot day, or I am too fat.

This is not what Tom thinks, though. The other day he was lying on the sofa, the way he does, with his legs all over the place, reading a book from the library, and he caught at her hand as she passed. Look here, Aly, he said. She knelt by his side and looked. She smiled when she saw the book was about *The Nude in Art*. As long as it's culture, she teased, and he smiled, and said, this reminds me of you. A woman with light reddish hair, lying in a pink haze. Renoir. His blues faded, so this didn't always look so pink, he told her knowledgeably, his fingers as he spoke tracing on the page the curve of breast and hip. But she's like you, all soft. I wish I could draw figures, Aly. I'd draw you, and it'd be even more beautiful than this. That he thinks she is beautiful and nothing of himself, it always amazes her. She said, you are beautiful, Tom, you are. No-one has ever painted anything like you. If I had any talent, I'd show you. Just then, bending over him, taking in the sweep of brow and the heart-stopping clarity of his eyes, and all down the harmonious sprawling length of him, she was struck by a kind of despair. Her resources—nothing specially fine or skilled—would always be inadequate to express a fraction of what she felt, even while at the same time thinking of some other quite everyday thing, whenever he was in her sight. No way she might try to show him could ever be other than ephemeral—as soon as done or uttered, lost! He would never know the whole of what she meant when she said, you are beautiful. Then Tom's book thudded to the floor, its pages splayed. Wordlessly, in a timeless, shameless male gesture, he pressed her hand hard and insistently down against him. And the feeling disappeared, in a burst of joy every bit as uncomplicated as what he wanted from her at that moment. Oh, this he shall have, this I can do! The easiest thing in the world!

The singer's gone, and the next item gets her full attention. No, surely— but it is. "Women Who Are in Love with Boys."

The women on the screen, right here. Thank heavens he's out! A teacher with big hair and slit mini-skirt—former teacher—a slattern of a neighbour, a sister-in-law! And the boys, just the kind you always find lurking where they shouldn't be, the ones the girls threw back. All complacently babbling away. It's like that old Monty Python TV game, "Spot the Brain Cell." How many of these people can there be? She's compelled to watch. When it's over, she sits there feeling as if she's been elbowed in a tender place by a stranger passing in the street. And then she starts to laugh. That's it! No Mum's best friend, why ever not? Go on TV! Don't leave anything out!—and she laughs, falling sideways on the sofa, till she can't laugh any more.

Then she gets up and takes a shower. She washes her hair. Puts on a clean dress, remembering how her mother always bathed and changed into a fresh cotton frock in the afternoon, for her father when he came in. An old-fashioned custom, predicated on women being at home, and much else. And her father's been gone a long time. Still, the memory of it pleases.

The doorbell rings. Has he forgotten his key?

It's Toby.

He's quite like himself; and at least she's wearing the clean dress, an elongated T-shirt. She wishes it were something more solid, and that she'd put her bra back on. He goes over to the mantelpiece where the mountain devils stand side by side. "I do remember these things. I had a Scotsman in a kilt. It's folk art really, isn't it?" he remarks heavily. "Well, Aly, what's to be done?"

It would sound dumb to say, don't call me Aly any more.

He strokes his chin. Paterfamilias. "This is very upsetting for us, and for Griselda," he says.

"I don't much like being in a soap opera with you, either." Feeble, and Toby disregards it.

"Let him come home, Aly. It would be healthier for the boy, and for his sister. You were fond of them both as children, weren't you? This is really just an aberration, you know. No harm done, a few wounded feelings, if it stops here. An experience we can all learn from. In future years—"

The key turns in the lock.

"What are you doing here?" says Tom.

"I'm talking to Aly."

"Now you're talking to me."

"I'm talking to Aly about what this is doing to your mother. And to me."

"Then you've got nothing to complain about," says Tom. "You should be grateful. We've brought you together."

Don't do this, Tom.

Toby turns to her. "What have you done to him?" he says, almost conversationally. "Couldn't you have just had it off quietly, given him his education, sent him back with a few finer points? No, you had to make a production out of it, and look at what we've got to deal with now."

Tom has gone rigid. In the same flat conversational tone, he says, "You hypocrite."

His father walks out.

Tom finds a way. There's a special course, mostly for older people who want to go to university, but also for kids who've failed their first try. "And dropouts and misfits generally," he says cheerfully. "The thing is," he adds, "I don't want the school to be able to hassle you any more. I don't want them to pay all that money for school fees any more, either. They can't make me stay at school, and I can do this by myself."

A short, curt conversation with Toby on the phone, and then all is quiet.

He gets a job in a fast-food restaurant up on the highway, at night. It's not so bad, he says, except for the hat. She goes up there to see, from the outside. She doesn't go in. The hat is ridiculous. He doesn't look ridiculous, he looks energetic. There are several boys and girls working there. Do Toby and Louise know he's here? She's half-afraid to meet them, also hovering, peeking through the window.

When he comes home, he smells of frying, and he's off hamburgers, he says, forever. He has a shower and then studies for a few hours more.

"Are you sure you can do all this?" she asks.

"Why not?" He doesn't even understand the question. He's happy not to be a schoolboy any more.

He goes to his lute lesson on Saturday mornings, before his shift at the restaurant, and though he can't practise as much as he used to, he always finds time to play on Sundays. How did she live through the weekends of that earlier life, without his music? His madrigals, his airs.

On her first day back at school, the Boss ambushes her as she signs in. "All right, Alyson?"

"Yes," she says, not meeting his eyes. At least no more will be heard from Tom's old school. That was what most concerned him, the Headmasters' relationship being touchy as between public and private. So perhaps it is all sorted out.

Nothing stays the same, though.

One Saturday afternoon she's working on a tub on the balcony, filling it with this and that, trying to achieve just the spilling-over effect she wants, when she hears a thumping on the stairs. She opens the door, and there he is searching for his keys, balancing an upended coffee table against the wall.

"Will you look at this, Aly!" he says. "I got it for a song, practically, at that place up on the highway! Isn't it excellent?" A real kidney-shaped coffee table. She could hardly dislike it more.

She's noticed this already, that to him Fifties design is a fascination. Anything leopard-skin, melamine or Day-Glo. It exists for him only as antiques. To her, it's the horrible stuff her mother couldn't afford to get rid of until it was scuffed and worn and even uglier than it started out. Unfortunately, he's interested in interiors as well as exteriors. The Italian architects he admires all design furniture, and he's probably got it in mind, too.

And now he thinks this is his home, and he can furnish it.

His excitement fades. "You hate it."

"I really, really hate it."

They've never argued about anything like this before. She tells him the table can't stay. He disparages her taste. He retreats behind his earphones, sunk in the chair he's referred to as floral junk. He's listening to rock music, she can tell because it's so loud it leaks tinnily out into the room. "You'll make yourself deaf!" she shouts. "So there!" He takes off the earphones to hear what she's saying, then puts them on again. You don't expect to get involved with a minor and spend time fighting over the decor. There are a lot of things you don't expect.

The table ends up by the mantelpiece with his library books on it.

He didn't stand over me, she thinks. He's tall, he could have. He didn't raise his voice to me. Of course, I gave in.

Then, one night he doesn't come straight home from the restaurant. He goes to a party with the kids who work there. When he finally gets in, very late, he's drunk. She gets up, meets him in her nightie. "Sorry, Aly," he mumbles, and lurches past her into the bathroom, where he's violently sick for a long time. Then he crawls into the bedroom and falls asleep. The bathroom's a disgusting mess, and she takes off her nightie and cleans it and then has a shower. The bedroom doesn't smell too good, either. She opens the window. He mumbles again, flings a heavy arm over her that she pushes away.

In the morning, he's ashamed, although he doesn't remember the worst of it. She tries not to be too outraged. She can't sound like a mother, she can't wag a finger and say, you have to learn. And he's not a child. He's someone who doesn't yet know the limits of what is possible. But if he did, he wouldn't be with her.

It doesn't happen again. He seems to have learned by himself.

"Do you think I should grow a moustache, Aly?" he asks. "It'd make me look older."

"No!" She's horrified. She doesn't say, that would really look ridiculous.

Things have settled down in one respect. There's only silent disapproval now, and, from Toby and Louise, what feels like silent threat. Nothing is actually happening, except for what's going on inside her head. She's doing it to herself.

Night is when it's worst. She can't stop the thoughts rolling around inside her skull, from side to side it seems, as she turns away from Tom to the edge of the bed, and back again towards him, where open-eyed she can dimly see his bright soft hair fallen over his forehead, feel the rhythm of his breathing on her face.

This particular night she gets up, puts on the light in the kitchen, makes camomile tea, sits at the table to drink it. Earlier in the evening she was working here; there's a stack of paper, and a pencil. She pulls a sheet towards her and draws a clumsy line down the middle of it. In the left column she writes the names of all the elderly leading men of Hollywood who still unfailingly get the girl. Other names. Pablo Casals married a student— what?—sixty years or so younger. A record, possibly, inconceivable in reverse. Unless you count *Harold and Maude*. Lovely little movie, but not quite the answer. Artists, of course, Picasso . . . High culture, pop culture, it makes no difference. This list could go on forever. On the right side, Mrs. Robinson. The actress hardly older than I am now, surely, and a beauty, but didn't she look ravaged? Her pencil jabs at the page. What was that one where the woman, with her son's roommate, in the elevator . . .? Forget it. Trash. Classics? *Der Rosenkavalier*. The Marschallin,

making losing sound great. Kate Chopin. What kind of sell-out
is that, *The Awakening*? She's still got to die! The French. Edith
Piaf shares her grave with a young man. A plus. Sort of a plus.
Chéri. Was he as young as Tom, Colette's Chéri? That terrible
scene where he sees her as she's finally become, grey and stout.
Shock, horror, unhappy ever after. Never mind Colette herself,
taken care of by a young husband till death. This plus is can-
celled out. Because the story she told is still pretty much the
only story.

Tom stands naked at the door of the bedroom, yawning and
rubbing his face. "Aly? What are you doing?"

"Nothing. Couldn't sleep. Do you want some tea?"

"No. Come back to bed."

She doesn't want him to see her tear up this crazy list, to think
it might be something. She slips it under the pile of papers, and
goes back to bed. She doesn't forget to throw it away in the
morning, but she doesn't look at it again. She doesn't have to.

It is a thing will soon decay, Then take the vantage whilst you
may, And this is love as I hear say.

He's seventeen.

CHAPTER EIGHT

It's been raining for weeks. Birds sit on the balcony rail preening wet feathers, or just gazing moodily out. There's only so many worms you can eat, he says. Spiders have started seeking refuge inside, big hairy ones coming out of the trees. He likes removing them for her in his bare hands and telling her they're harmless, which she knows.

He's got tonight off from the restaurant to go to a recital given by his lute teacher, in a small hall not far away. He's late getting home. Maybe they went out after that to eat. Not drink. Not when he's taken the bike.

She's finished her work, watched the late-night movie. More rain. She goes into the bathroom to close the window where the rain spits in, picks up a wet towel he's let fall to the floor. Oh, Tom.

She walks around for a while, from room to room. It is late.

His teacher's name she knows, and more or less where he lives. The problem is there are two people with that name in the phone book, in the same area. It's after one o'clock. What if she wakes some total stranger? Who will she say she is?

By one forty-five she doesn't care. She rings the first number. Wrong. Sorry to disturb you. "'Sorright," croaks a sleepy voice.

At the second, a woman answers, not sleepy but sharp, as people are if they're up late, expecting not a social call but a death, a pervert. She stumbles out her question. The concert tonight, your husband . . . Tom Gabrielli, who lives with me? A man comes on. "Who is this?"

Tom Gabrielli, he lives with me.

"What? Tom went home after— we had coffee— that must have been about eleven, half past. This isn't Louise?"

No. Thank you. Sorry to disturb you.

She stands in the middle of the room thinking of Louise, how she'd call all the hospitals.

He's broken down, far from a phone. The phones never work when you need them, they've been vandalized or choked with coins. He'll come in, all wet, and she'll reproach him. Oh Tom, I was thinking of hospitals, thinking of the police. He'll kiss her, not laugh at her, because it's very late, he knows that, she's not being unreasonable. He'll make promises that he'll keep next time if he possibly can. She will forget how this felt. This waiting.

She's still standing there, however much later, wringing her hands. Which is not what she does in real life. The feeling is a pounding throughout her whole body. Something must happen. She must hear.

The doorbell. The door, much further away than she realised.

"Is this where Thomas Gabrielli lives? Are you his mother?"

He lives with me. She doesn't know if she says it or not, if any sound comes out.

The policeman glances down at the paper in his hand, notes the age. "Landlady?"

She simply looks at him. Begs him to speak, not to speak.

Wet road, he says. Windy corner. Dog or possum, probably.

Strangely, she hears herself ask, is the other driver all right?

That's good, because Tom would feel terrible if he'd hurt another person.

"Give you a lift up to the hospital," he says.

Think. Think of Louise.

"I've got to call his parents."

No answer, and the machine's not on. If it were, what would she say?

She grabs her purse.

"Umbrella?" says the policeman. "It's wet out there. Windy, too."

This part of the hospital is brightly lit. An ambulance stands under the portico, and a stretcher is being carried in. "All right, love," says an ambulance man to the patient on the stretcher. "Almost there now." A twisted uncomprehending face, white hair in curlers. Run.

The job of everyone is to slow her down. To point her in a different direction, show her a different stairwell, a row of chairs.

The doctors are wearing suits, there must have been a dinner, the kind where speeches are made. It is, was Saturday night. Tall, dark men, in good suits and prime of life, talking to each other in energetic undertones.

"You're his mother?"

The knee's broken, several places, bone through the skin. Bruising, kidneys, not a real problem. What might be a problem, the head injuries, in spite of the helmet, the angle. CAT scan.

His beautiful brain, full of music and buildings and motor-bikes and sex. Nothing in it of meanness. Nothing about picking up towels, not a single thing.

There's a phone in the corridor.

Above the telephone is a painting. Its bright hard-edged stripes, meant to cheer, hurt her eyes. Toby says, "Just got in. *La Traviata*, supper. What the hell— Alyson?"

∞

They bring him back, she stands by his bed.

"Still out," says the nurse. "Until we know, try not to worry too much."

How much would that be?

There are bandages, and under them she can see his head has been shaved. She rests her hand gently on his, and for the first time ever nothing happens. A bare foot sticks out from under the sheet. No-one's looking. She bends and kisses it.

Louise in black silk trousers and sequinned jacket of many deep colours is a lustrous moth drawn to the light that falls around the bed.

All these people who've come to Tom's bed are dressed up, it's an occasion.

"You're the mother?" The nurse's eyes flick from one to the other.

"I'm the mother," says Louise.

The CAT scan shows no real damage. Needs to be watched, of course. Lucky, lucky, lucky. Tom is a very lucky boy. Go home, they say.

Out in the corridor sits his grandmother, Maura, with Griselda, in her night-out best, dozing on her shoulder. Maura unfolds her long legs, stiffly stands. Griselda springs up, holding tight to her hand. Lucky, says Toby. Very lucky, says Maura gravely.

"Lucky! Lucky?" Louise cries, low and hoarse. "What was he doing out on the road on a Saturday night, in the middle of the night, in the wind and rain, an inexperienced rider, what was he doing?"

"Darling," says Maura.

Louise shakes off her mother's hand. "What was he doing?"

Not far away, it wasn't far, she wants to say, but the question has already been through her head a thousand times and that isn't the answer. What was he doing out?

"Darling, he's all right—"

"He's all right! How can you say that? He's all right? Is this what you call all right? She's taken my son, and not content with that, she's let this thing happen! His leg smashed! His head! He almost died! You know her! You know how she's envied me, little Alyson, envied me my career, my house, my husband. All these years. Envied me my son, the thing I love most in the world! You've told me she means no harm. Now, *now* do you see?"

Griselda's face has gone empty. Maura puts an arm around her. "Think, Louise."

"Think! Have I done anything but think? About where he is, what he's doing! About how his life has been screwed up, his chances, his dreams, everything. About how I gave birth to him, cleaned up his shit, sat up all night with him while he struggled for breath—his asthma!—suffered with him, watched over him, and now I'm the one who spied on him, the one who doesn't want him to have what he wants, the one who has to watch him through a window making hamburgers, who has to hear it from *her* when he's hurt! Think! All this time I've been thinking, and have you been supportive of me, any more than you have through the rest of my life? Answer me that!"

"I can't say everything you do and say is right, Louise, even to be supportive, whatever that means. This is not right. Tom isn't going to die, he's young, he'll mend, he's still your son. Everyone here has reason to be grateful for Tom's life. Let's go home."

"You include her? You dare to say to me she has reason, she has a right? This monster of selfishness, who's not fit to—"

Kiss his feet.

She's walking away down the corridor.

"Louise, this is too much."

"Does she think he'll never leave her? It's a matter of time! Is she so stupid? Is she insane?"

The voices are not low enough. The tone is unmistakable.

A burly young male nurse passes her, going purposefully in the opposite direction. "Right-oh, folks," she hears him say. "We're all very upset, but this is not the time or the place.

There's sick people here, don't forget. Go home and get a good morning's sleep. Out."

The sky just before dawn is as clear and grey as Tom's eyes when he wakes.

She stands under the portico, and they pass her without a word. From the silent car park, Toby's voice: "Get *in*, Griselda!" The slam of a door, a screech of tyres on the wet road. Tom's tyres screeching on the curve, Tom flying sideways. He ended up on one side of the road, the bike on the other, said the policeman. The bike's a write-off.

A car draws up in front of her. Maura leans over and opens the door. "Do you need a lift, Alyson?"

"A policeman brought me."

"Get in."

Maura's third husband, the one who died playing tennis with Tom, left her a very wealthy woman, according to Toby. As opposed to her second, who left her only a moderately wealthy woman, and her first, who left her Louise.

The car is a wealthy woman's car.

"I have to concentrate on the driving," says Maura. "I'm not young any more and I'm done in." An unnecessary warning. To speak of Tom now would be to break down utterly. To speak of Louise, unthinkable.

Maura looks like Tom. A sideways glance. Tom looks like her. The clean line of cheek and jaw-bone, it's still there in his grandmother, framed in silver. The last time I saw them together, Tom's face wouldn't yet have shown it, and in any case I wouldn't have noticed or cared.

She gives directions off the highway—left here, no, sorry, right—to her street, her building.

Maura looks up. "So this is where Tom's been living. I could have found out. I did think about coming over."

From some unknown place in her brain comes a coherent utterance. "You would have been welcome."

"I should have come. But you weren't lonely."

"No."

"Alyson, I had three husbands. Louise lost her father early. I travelled a lot and left her behind, I brought new men into her life. Two stepfathers. Louise holds on to what she's got. I do accept some responsibility for what happened outside Tom's room tonight—this morning. I really can't say any more. I can't apologise."

"I don't expect it."

"No, you don't, do you?"

The currawongs are warbling in the trees all around. Her feet, and the bottoms of her old blue jeans, as she stands on the grass verge watching the big car slowly round the corner, are wet from the night's rain.

Coherent still, she calls the hospital. No change. It's too soon. It is implied that she is being a pest, and probably Louise is being a pest, too.

She takes off her clothes and drops them on the floor, as Tom does, pulls the curtains, lies down. Each breath brings a new fear. What if the doctors were wrong? What if after all he's not all right? What if, now they've sent her home, he takes a turn for the worse? Will anyone call her? No, he could die, and no-one would ever call her. Not till too late. She should never have left him! Incredibly, she dozes. Wakes. Sleeps again, fitfully. Sleeping, her hand moves. Of itself, it searches the empty side of the bed, and not once but several times she sits up suddenly, in a sick panic. Where's Tom? It's light already, and he's not home!

Call again. The new shift has come on. Someone as brisk but not without warmth. He's regained consciousness, he's sleeping.

She lies staring, wide awake.

He knows nothing of all that happened. Thank God.

What Louise said. I haven't envied her career, that's not true. Nor the house nor Toby, though he had his reasons for letting her think so, nor Tom nor Griselda. No, Griselda wasn't mentioned.

I have envied the fact that she's never made a bad move, that things have always turned out for her, I have. I would have admitted it. Is it so terrible?

That wasn't why I wanted Tom. I began to see him as himself. He saw me.

As for the rest. Louise is not wrong.

Louise's car is in the hospital car park. She goes away, drives around. Comes back. Still there. Has tea in the hospital cafeteria. People in dressing gowns, people trailing drips, pushing walking frames, encumbered by other wheeled and tubed contraptions. A world of its own that you forget is here when you don't have to be. Is Louise going to be with him all day? What if she is? What if I can't see him at all? But I can. I can just go up. And then what?

The car is gone.

There are flowers by his bed. "I didn't bring flowers," she says.

His lip is split, but he says: "Come closer."

She puts her ear to his mouth. "You're a flower," he whispers. "You're pretty, you smell so nice."

The man in the other bed gets up and leaves.

She covers the palm of his hand with kisses.

∞

This is the routine. Louise comes in the morning. Maura, not every day, in the afternoon, as a buffer. Alyson from school. Toby brings Griselda after work.

Tom has pyjamas. He had pyjamas all along, of course. He just didn't bring them to her place, not seeing the need, and Louise has brought them for him now. Louise takes them home and washes them, too.

She meets his lute teacher, who gets up and gives her the visitor's chair, and leaves as soon as he can. One afternoon a school friend he's seen sometimes at the pool, who leaves even faster.

A young resident comes by, leans her elbows on the end of the bed. "So the catheter's out," she says. "Having any trouble weeing?"

Tom smiles broadly, shakes his head. The pyjamas are blue, his eyes are blue. When the doctor pulls up his pyjama top and leans over his chest with her stethoscope, Alyson looks away.

Weekends are harder. She still looks for the cars but sometimes she misses them, and then there's overlap. One afternoon she comes in and sees Louise sitting there, back to the door. She just goes away, and waits.

Tom says to her when she returns, "Don't do that, Aly."

He doesn't know.

∞

As time goes on, he becomes bad-tempered. He's not sunny or philosophical any more. He hates his cast, of some more high-tech material than the plaster she remembers, he hates the way his hair is growing back in tufts. She's brought his books, and a couple of his teachers have come to see him with advice, but he's not studying. He's beside himself with frustration.

Toby comes to see her again, and this time he knows she'll be alone.

"I admit I was frightened, Alyson, as frightened as I've ever been. You too. Don't think I underestimate that."

This is a confiding Toby. "I haven't had it as easy all my life as you think I have," he tells her when she's given him a beer. "I had a drunken sot for a father, a bitter mother. Tom knows this. Has he said? No? Well, he's young, he's got other things to talk about. I'm not trying to get under your guard, I just wanted to say, when he was born he was the best thing that had ever happened to me. I wanted to give him everything in the world. Louise—she is his mother. About the night of the accident, Alyson—you can't blame her, can you? She does say terrible things. She's said a few of them to me on occasion. But she was very emotional."

Yes, she was.

"Now, we've got to talk. About Tom's future. You say it's up to him. But he's *seventeen*, Aly. This is a turning point in his life."

"Seventeen—but there are kids younger than Tom that are—" What was it she wanted to say? "Homeless kids, and prostitutes." Toby tucks his chin into his neck in order to look at her over his glasses in a reproving way. What has this to do with Tom? He's joined his hands together in front of him. He doesn't look like Toby the philanderer, he looks like the judge he might some day be. She struggles on down this diversion. Once she and Tom saw a documentary on TV about child combatants in the Liberian civil war, little kids riding tanks, waving huge guns. "They die in wars," she says.

"Nevertheless, Aly. Hardly the point. In view of what's happened. It's a set-back, at a crucial time. He's not studying, you can see that. He'll need to work bloody hard to catch up, and even then it'll be touch and go. He'll need a long course of physiotherapy, with that kind of injury. Now you know he wants to do something very difficult. It's all he's ever wanted, to be an architect. He needs his maths, that's where he's weak. Did you realise that?"

He can tell she didn't, that Tom never confessed it to her, and she can tell it pleases him. One up. And yet, she thinks, there are things I know about Tom that they have no idea of. There is a part of him that is inaccessible to them and always will be, but they can't afford to admit it now.

"It's by no means certain he can do it, Aly, after this. What if he fails? How will he feel then?"

She gets up, goes to the balcony door to look out. He won't have to see her face to know that the point has gone home.

"He's given up a lot for this adventure. School—and make no mistake, he was happy there till you came along. His friends, and he had some good ones. You can't tell me he's keeping up with his music the way he used to. He's making hamburgers when he should be studying. He's got the stress of this problem with Louise. Look at Griselda, she's suffering, too, don't think she isn't, he feels responsible. And now there's a good chance he'll fail his exams. He'll regret it, Aly. He's never had to regret anything in his life before, but he'll regret this. He might not blame you openly, he'd be loyal, but what do you think he'll feel deep down, when he's a bit older and realises what he's done? What a mistake he's made."

He hasn't said a thing she hasn't thought herself.

She feels terribly, terribly tired.

It's not only Toby.

Tom is alive, miraculously alive. She has no right to want more.

How to justify the risk of doing him more harm, when so much has already been done, in the name of something that must—it isn't as if she hasn't always known it—inevitably end? That from the day it began has been, hour by hour, ending. No. That has, in a split second on a wet road, ended.

It's just that he hasn't realised it yet. He's the only one.

In a trance, this Sunday, she gets up, dresses, drives to the hospital.

Let there be a reason.

When she gets to Tom's room, the other bed is empty. Had someone been in it, there might have been a reprieve. One more day.

There is no reason.

Tom is sitting on the edge of his bed. A pair of aluminium crutches rests by his outstretched leg in its fraying cast.

"I'm getting the hang of it," he says. "I'll be out of here soon."

She sits down at his other side.

He must see it in her face.

"Don't, Aly," he says.

"Tom, you have to go home."

"We've had this conversation. I'm not talking about it any more."

"You almost died. You didn't, you're alive, that's the important thing. Now you've got to do what you always wanted to do. I don't want you to fail."

"What the fuck are you talking about? Fail? I'm not going to fail!"

She stands, trembling all over. "I've thought and thought, Tom."

"You don't know how! You've lost your nerve!"

"It's for the best. It is." For your own good.

"How can you be so stupid, Aly!" He's shouting now. "This is a terrible mistake!"

He's tired, too. He's had a lot of pain. Under his eyes are dark smudges. She can see them now because his face is so white. She's never seen him so pale, not the day she took him home from the station, not the night his parents found out. And the boy who never cried is crying. She tries to take his hand, but he's brushing furiously at his eyes and reaching for his crutches. He means to follow her. But he's too clumsy yet, one of them clatters to the floor, and she leaves him. She runs away.

Down the long corridor. The lift is full. She stands facing the door with her eyes tight shut. Out into the car park. She's unable to remember the number of the bay where her car is parked. She comes upon it by chance. She sits there with her head on the wheel while cars come and go around her, until someone looking for a space calls, "You all right? Staying or going?" She raises her head, turns uncomprehendingly towards the sound. When he sees her face, he says hastily, "Take your time," and draws away. He probably thinks someone's died.

Toby comes with Griselda. Alyson has collected Tom's smaller things and put them in his backpack, by the door. There are the same boxes he brought with him. A few more books, including the one she gave him for Christmas. Larger items of clothing she's laid on the sofa. Griselda silently carries shirts and jackets on hangers down to the car. She doesn't look at Alyson, who sits on the balcony, quite still, her eyes fixed on a point just above the horizon.

Clouds. No, smog.

It's not enough that the thing happens. There always has to be the removal of the remains, the disposal of the effects.

Toby comes to the balcony door. He's holding Tom's lute. He says, "You know you're doing the right thing. It's for his own good." He bends to kiss her goodbye, and his lips brush hers. "You're a lovely woman, Aly."

Her head jerks away and for an instant every nerve end in her body prickles with revulsion. But the effect is as soon lost. She's too tired to care what he means by it, she can't be bothered being demeaned.

She says only, "Don't call me that," and resumes looking out.

CHAPTER NINE

For a week she's had swollen eyelids, blotches on her cheeks and throat. If he came back now, he wouldn't know her.

She puts the ballerina back in her box, with the red devil. She leaves it open, goes around collecting things. His love letter. Christmas and birthday cards, and the untied ribbons she never should have kept in the first place. What was she thinking of? Setting herself up for this. The CD he gave her. She'll never play it again. *Lagrime mie.* As soon have her heart torn out and listen to her own screams. The photo of them both, that lovely foolish photo, that up till now has been by the bed. There were other photos that he kept among his own things, in envelopes, labelled "Aly on Beach" and so on; these, without looking, she put in among his books, where now nobody will have reason to search for them, to send back home to him. What he will do with them she cannot know. She adds to the box the *Young Man Against a Background of Flames*. Everything. Then she stands on a chair and hides it from herself in the deepest part of the highest shelf in her wardrobe.

She clears the mantelpiece, rehangs all her pictures, changes everything. Still she sees him everywhere. They didn't take his coffee table. She didn't think of giving it to them, because she's got used to its being where it is. There's no place to hide a coffee table. She takes his books back to the library and pays the fine.

In the bottom of the laundry basket, neglected since she's been going back and forth to the hospital, she finds some of his underwear. She sits on the edge of the bath with it in her hands. It's not particularly erotic, like women's underwear is supposed to be for men. It's washing. That he did himself, but only when he'd run completely out of underpants. An awful coffee table and a bunch of dirty underwear. Tom.

A student collapses in her class. Year Nine. He's standing at the blackboard writing the answers to some questions on behalf of his group, and suddenly he staggers, and falls, just like that, clutching theatrically at the chalk shelf. At first she thinks it's one of the idiotic things they do, then she panics, runs out of the room herself looking for help. This is not handling it very well, by any standards.

Afterwards Bill says, "You hadn't touched him? Good. That's the main thing."

Then he tells a long story about how once, years ago, he tapped a kid on the head with a forefinger, and the kid fell down frothing at the mouth. "Had a soft spot on his head or something, no-one knew. Just a little tap with a finger," he concludes. "The parents weren't too bad about it. Fortunately for yours truly."

"Just a little tap," says Mel sceptically.

She only half-listens. At least the kid's all right.

At home, she sits at the table for hours correcting the same number of papers she could have done in forty minutes, before. It's this tiredness.

On TV, there are commercials about what to do with your superannuation lump sum when you retire. You roll it over, that's what they say, then you buy a van and drive around the country, you hug your partner on top of a mountain in some National Park. The money's not going to be a problem. It's twenty-five years away. What on earth does one do with twenty-five years? That's her question.

She hears nothing. After all these months of being with him every day, there's total silence. How it would be, this silence, how it would eat into her, is something she couldn't have imagined.

Katie knows no more than she does. Louise is being very tight-lipped, she says.

Then, one afternoon, out shopping for food—more from habit than inclination—she sees Griselda mooching along on the other side of the street with a bulging sports bag slung over her shoulder. She mooches rather fast, and Alyson has to run to catch up with her. "Griselda! Griselda!"

She must look odd: red-faced and out of breath. Griselda doesn't meet her eyes at first. Uneasily, she puts down her bag, pulls at the skirt of her school uniform.

No preliminaries. "Tom. How is he?"

Griselda shrugs. "This very moment? I dunno."

"He's at home, then."

"Not really. He is and he isn't."

Alyson wants to take her by the shoulders and shake her. But once Griselda gets going, she tells. "He didn't actually come home. He said he wouldn't, I knew he wouldn't. He always means what he says. He said he'd go to Grandma's, and she let him. She's got a room in the garden. So we had to move everything again before he got out of hospital. I'm sick of lugging his stuff around. Mum and Dad were ropeable, really. He's having physiotherapy and swimming in the heated pool at the hospital, and studying like a maniac to make up what he missed. Grandma and Mum aren't speaking." She scratches her calf with the heel of her sneaker. "It's not all your fault, Aly, I don't think. I'm trying to be fair here."

"Thank you, Griselda." Gratefully, Griselda escapes.

He didn't go home.

She thinks of calling him. She thinks of it for days on end. Now she knows where he is. Maura would let her speak to him. If he would speak to her. It would be wrong to ask him to. He's supposed to heal, to work. Let him be. That's the whole point. It's done.

The couple opposite have moved out. Together? She has no idea. She couldn't care less.

Her own place is very quiet and tidy.

Often when she comes home, just before she puts her key in the lock, she thinks of something she might say to him. Or she imagines she hears him playing, expects to open the door and see him there, looking up from his music.

More than once when Tom played, when he was getting it right, she saw on his face an expression that had something in it of a look that might be there when they made love. Sometimes, his fingers finding what they wanted in the strings, he even made a sound in his throat that was an echo of those other sounds that being inside her brought him to. For Tom, to make perfect music was like coming, or was it the other way round, that to him coming was like music? Not was. Is, oh God, is. She thinks: if I let it into my head again, this specific thing, I might die of it.

In the middle of the night, when control is relinquished to sleep, she's vulnerable. Sometimes she seems to wake up to his voice. Aly. Aly, she's heard him say, softly. And been more desolate than ever in her life before to find herself alone in the bed.

The woman above, the one who gave Tom a funny look the day he waited for her on the stairs, a woman she hardly knows, and has never spoken to about anything but the business of the building, says to her one morning, "I miss your son's music."

"He doesn't live here any more."

She doesn't say, he wasn't my son, don't you have eyes? He was my lover.

One day her car's in dock again, and she gets the train, and realises it's the same train. When she gets off at her station, she sees the Sikh guard in his turban leaning out of his window in the last carriage. He's watching her get off, where the gap is wide. He needs no more accidents. She half-nods to him, she wants him to remember her, that she was once with Tom, but at first he gives no sign. Then, as the train pulls out, he smiles in recognition.

We weren't lonely, she thinks, but only strangers knew us.

Katie "needs space" from Brian, and has borrowed a house down the South Coast for the weekend. It's an old-fashioned weekender, just across from a beach where there's nobody else but a few surfers. They spend the day lying around reading, swim a bit, buy some fish and some oysters. At night they sit on the verandah and get drunk.

"They want menopausal women to give up sex now," grumbles Katie. "Healthiest, longest-lived women ever. They want you to garden—well, all right for you, you would anyway. Community activist—why not, I mean all that recycling just crying out, but *instead of?* Wise crone. Crone, I ask you! Rather cut my throat and be done with it than be that wise."

"Won't have to worry about that," says Alyson. "Not a problem."

Katie laughs hard. "Know what? The story is you seduced Tom and sort of kept him prisoner, and he had his accident making a break for it. I contradict it at every turn, naturally."

The stars are swaying in the sky. Alyson closes her eyes.

"Got a question for you," says Katie. "Maybe now's OK to ask. A boy of that age. Is it true?"

Alyson gets up and walks inside. In the spotty mirror hanging in the hallway her cheeks are an ugly, drunken red. Yes. Oh yes. All true.

Katie comes in, stumbling. "Sorry," she says. "Really. Oh I'm sorry, Aly. Know how you feel. I do. I hate Louise, too. Her and her gorgeous husband, the bastard, her perfect children. I really hate her."

Next morning, they are both very subdued.

Katie has decided to get a divorce.

Alyson has nothing to decide.

In the plant shop, it's peaceful. Cool, damp, green. The smell of earth and moss and peat and fertilizer makes her calmer. Sometimes she talks to the woman who owns the place, a sensible-looking woman in an apron that has pockets for twine and secateurs. One day this woman says to her, "You know something about plants, don't you?" She interrupts herself to snatch a crushed leaf out of the mouth of a passing toddler. "Not poisonous," she assures the mother, with a brisk smile. "That's all I need, a lawsuit," she says when they're out of hearing.

"I was brought up in a nursery. My father was a wholesale rose grower."

The woman makes a thoughtful face. "You don't want a part-time job, do you?"

"I'm a teacher."

"Pity, it's hard to get decent people. Even in times like these."
It's like a sign. Not that she believes in signs.

In the staff room, Bill's bragging about his son, the future
Wallaby scrum-half. "Fifteen last birthday, but you should see
the brawn on him! Thighs like this!" And adds, aside, "Not your
type, Alyson. Sorry." She hasn't looked up from her work, but
feels the group melt away. Leaving her with one thought:
another sign.

She's stayed stubbornly all these years with a wrong choice.
She's shown she can, for what it's worth. Enough is enough. It's
funny, not so long ago, this would have been a huge decision.
Now it's simply something she's doing. She quits.

She'll work through to the end of the year, and then she'll take
all the money that's coming to her, mostly accrued long-service
pay, and put it in the bank. For what, she has no idea.

"You're not very big," says Tania, the woman in the apron.
"That's the only thing. Can you do heavy lifting? Bags of fertilizer, pallets of seedlings, stacks of pots?"

"I think so," she says. When you do physical work, you sleep.

Her senior students have taken their exams. Tom has taken
his. He will not have failed.

When the kids ask if she's coming back next year, she says she doesn't know. She just wants to go quietly away. Some of them wish her Merry Christmas. Tiffany is somewhat restrained, but seems to bear no grudge. She must know how it turned out. She's been seen around with a boy who's a Sufi, and has declared an interest in changing her name to something more spiritual.

Mel, watching her pack her things in boxes, says in an undertone, "This wasn't necessary."

"It's not that. It never came naturally to me, Mel."

Bill overhears the last part and says, without humour, "We can't all be Superteacher."

The Boss wishes her well, "In all your future endeavours."

She's lost weight. This time, when she goes up North for Christmas, her mother is so anxious that she doesn't say much at all, just feeds her.

That she's quit teaching isn't what worries them.

"I never thought you were cut out for it," says her mother.

"Superannuation's overrated," says her stepfather. "Get your own little business, be your own boss. That's the way to go. There's your bugs and disasters, don't have to tell you that. Plants won't ever make you rich, but they'll repay you as long as you live." He's keen to teach her, and at last she finds herself wanting something again, to learn.

∞

She's not sure how it happens—perhaps it's because they're sitting at the kitchen table with a pot of tea and a plate of biscuits and it's a hot night, crickets making a racket outside, moths whirring into the screens, and the drone of a sports programme on the TV in the next room, interspersed with bursts of cheering and her stepfather's muffled shouts of encouragement, and her mother's in her dressing gown, and all this puts her off her guard— but she starts to cry. Her mother says, "Sweetheart, what is it?" And she tells. No, not all, but enough.

The shouting stops, and her stepfather wanders in from the living room.

"What's all this bawling in aid of?" he complains. "A man can't watch the fights in peace."

"Love," replies her mother.

"You got the full story?" He pulls up a chair.

A smile interrupts Alyson's tears here and there at the way her mother tells it, she can't help it. He listens in silence, except for: "Come again? *How* old?"

When the story's finished, her mother leans over, caresses Alyson's hair. She smells of lily of the valley talc. Alyson, as a child, has often bought a flowery cylinder of this same powder in its special beribboned Mother's Day cellophane at the chemist's, wrapped it in paper with more flowers on it, presented it and had it received as the greatest surprise in the world.

"You've been a very silly girl," says her mother.

"So I've been told. I don't need to hear it again, Mum."

"Oh, well then," says her mother in a hurt tone.

Her stepfather clears his throat. "I think your mother means," he says mildly, "to give in."

"That's what I do mean."

It's almost shocking.

"The mountains," says her mother judiciously, "That was naughty. But goodness me, there's been a lot of naughtiness in the mountains over the years."

Her stepfather smiles, but says nothing.

"The whole thing's unusual, I'll give you that. Still, he sounds like a nice, sensible boy."

"On the precocious side," remarks her stepfather.

"He'd have to be, to deal with parents like his. I remember them well, Dr. Know-all and Mr. God's Gift, QC."

Alyson laughs, licking a tear from her lip.

"No-one would be good enough for their boy, not if he was forty-six. I know this sort of people," she says, sketching expansively in the air with her free hand an invisible habitation of towers and quadrangles. "Broad-minded enough when it suits them, yes, but you touch their own interests and see what happens."

"A farmer with an open gate and a blue-ribbon bull calf gone missing wouldn't be in it," agrees her stepfather. "Only they'll come at you with words instead of a shotgun."

"But I was her friend. I didn't think at all about how she'd feel."

"Of course you didn't. You were in love."

It seems never to have occurred to anybody else who has spoken to her, except perhaps to cool-headed Maura, that this might be so. Her mother, with two gentle words, has opened wide the door to a cell in which she's spent too many solitary days and nights.

"Yes," she says, almost inaudibly, "I was."

"You would have thought. You would have tried to make it right eventually. Any parents'd be shocked. It'd need time. But they didn't give it any time at all, did they? And they were supposed to be your friends. It goes both ways. They could have given you some benefit of the doubt, and they could have told themselves it might be worse. They didn't have to like it but they could have tried. Even if they were only sitting it out. Instead they worked themselves up and they went on the attack from the beginning, and they waited their chance, didn't they? I know you. You'd do your best to stand your ground, but you'd be on the defensive." Her stepfather's nodding agreement. "You wouldn't fight, would you? And when he was hurt, that was their moment."

"Louise was unreachable, Mum, she'd scream at me, then Toby, he'd come and he'd—"

"Strategy."

"What?"

"Aly, he's the lawyer. You of all people should know that. What am I going to do with you? Their emotions are tools to them. They learn it, like anybody learns anything. Didn't we see Eric turn it on and off with you? Just what did you think he was doing, when he did that?"

Her fingernails deepen the scratches on the table. They saw Eric hit this table with his fist one night, turkey-cock red in the face, those cold bright eyes. The next moment, all disarming again. Not about anything very much, just keeping in shape. I am so stupid.

"You thought you'd put it all behind you," says her mother sadly. "But they know you. They know you can't take abuse, they know your history."

Alyson looks up, appalled.

Through everything that happened, for all that time, Toby was appearing in court in his silk and his wig, and Louise was supervising doctoral theses, and serving on curriculum panels, and writing her thing about "The Signification of the Phallus in *Troilus and Criseyde*," or whatever. They were both functioning, not out of control. Not either of them. Not Louise.

"I'm not saying they weren't truly upset," says her mother. "But love, you let them bamboozle you."

Yes, I'm an imbecile, she thinks. I must have it written all over me.

"You've got to know yourself," her stepfather says. "Next time you see your opportunity, don't let them get near you, Aly. What you do, come out of your corner dancing."

"That's the way," confirms her mother. "Though I do hate these rough games."

CHAPTER TEN

$\mathcal{M}$aura sounds older. Alyson hears, or imagines she hears, she's so on edge waiting for it, not only a fragility but a hesitation.

"My dear, he isn't with me any more." Where is he? It had to come, the time when he'd be somewhere I can't picture him. "He's found a place near the university. The phone—there is a phone. Last month they forgot to pay the bill, the young people, and it was cut off, but now it's . . . You know, he's almost never there. He seems to be so—"

"You could ask him if he'd mind," she blurts out.

But Maura says, "No. I think he'd be happy to hear from you, Aly," and gives her not only the number but the address too, from memory.

What makes her think he'd be happy? She called me Aly. She

wants to ask, did he talk about me? But she can't, and Maura doesn't offer more.

She calls several times. He's not there, no-one's there. Her resolve fails. She stops trying for a while.

Next time, someone answers, a girl, but he's out. The girl's apathy makes it impossible to find out when he'll be back. She's not asked if there's a message, but she wouldn't leave one anyway. Or the next time, when a boy shouts, without taking his mouth from the receiver, "Tom here? No. Sorry."

It's weeks before she can make herself try again. The second time, she hears the yell, "For you!" The phone seems to be in a hall, there are footsteps, but not his, voices, a slammed door. Then the sound of someone running down stairs. She might have heard a murmur: it's that woman again. Or maybe not. She hardly knows what she hears any more. She feels rather sick.

Forget it. Put down the phone.

It's his voice.

Maura was wrong. He's not happy, though he's terribly polite. How is he? Well, living here. How is it? It's not bad, a few people. Not from architecture, found it from a notice board. It's cheap. Working part-time doing odd jobs in Oliver's office. Copying, helping with models. Paper and Styrofoam.

"For a modernist?"

"It's a job," he says, and she hears no smile.

It seems to be an effort, but he asks her, how are you. She tells him about the plant shop. On and off, when they need me. Something full-time's opening up soon. I'm thinking about taking a proper course in horticulture, and eventually—

That's good, he says. He thanks her for calling.

She drives past the house. It's one of those places that's escaped gentrification by quite a long way. The iron lace has long ago been sold or rusted off and not replaced by anything, except upstairs where the verandah looks like it was closed in with glass louvres and plywood in about 1962.

Next time, she parks around the corner and walks by. Someone's feeding a cat. There's a cracked saucer with a waxy yellow rim around it by the front door.

Louise must be really worried about drugs now. Serves her right.

What she's doing has a nasty name. Or it would have, if he knew and if she knew for sure how he felt about it. If he hated it, if she knew that, there's a law against it. That must be how it works. But he doesn't know. She's got to know this at least, how he feels about it. And so much more. But probably that's how all the mad people who do these things think.

Poor woman. Take out an order against her.

This is not useful.

She thinks, I've never been a risk-taker, not really. I didn't know Eric was dangerous. And after him, I wanted only not to let myself be hurt ever again. When I met Tom, everything changed. I learned that that there are rewards that are worth any risk. Then I wavered, fumbled, fell. Now I have no choice but to do this, alone. And what I'm most afraid of is how he might look at me.

She parks across the road from the house. If he should come in or out—say, with a girl, or anyone—she'll go. He won't even see her. Then she'll come back again. As often as it takes.

It's been almost a year. He's eighteen. That sounds quite old to her now.

An old car, a smallish rustbucket, parks behind her. She doesn't notice it, she's gazing down the street in the direction she thinks, for no reason at all, he might come.

He's standing beside her window.

"I've given up motorbikes," he says.

She gets out.

He's grown the moustache he talked of, and a short beard too. His hair is cropped all over, most of its fairness gone. It's how much he is the same that makes it hard to speak.

"You've got a cat," she says on the doorstep.

"Comes with the house. Still a stray."

He picks up some mail lying at their feet, tosses it on the table where the phone is.

He kisses her. It's a peck on the cheek, such as he'd give his mother, or Maura, or Griselda if they came to visit. Yet he didn't kiss her in the street, as he would them. That's something they never did. The moustache isn't as silky as it looks.

He takes her into the kitchen. "What kind of tea? There's all these herby things. Ginseng, even."

"Just tea."

The smell of student houses hasn't changed much. Stir-fry, spilt beer, unlined trashbin, unwashed dishcloth, stale potpourri in a cereal bowl, candle, a whiff of controlled substance. Less patchouli and incense than there used to be, more aromatherapy going on.

The front door opens. A girl wanders in. She's very thin. "Did you see my psych notes? In a grungy green folder?" She sits down at the table, closes her eyes, rests her head on her hand. Can she be going to stay? She clearly sees no purpose in being introduced. At least this is not a girl he's interested in. Borderline anorexic, by the look of the arms, and completely self-involved. Dull, incomprehensible girl. To be in the same house with him, and not to care. Go away. Please.

She watches him making the tea. The beard is trimmed, it has a shape, it covers the right amount, it's not a fringe or a mat. She doesn't like it. Then she thinks again. This is also a look, meant to be tougher. With boots. It downplays his beauty, but maybe it does suit him, too. And it looks familiar.

"How's Griselda?"

"She's given up karate. Dislocated her shoulder, and after that it kept happening." He puts a mug of tea in front of her, and one in front of the girl, who murmurs thanks. "It was just a weakness in her, so she couldn't keep on with it."

Nothing compared to the weakness in me.

The girl takes her tea and goes.

Brighten up. She looks at the old enamelled stove. "There's enough of the Fifties here for you."

"Never walk out here in bare feet, the floor's filthy."

He has this terse way of speaking that he didn't have before. Well, that's what happens when they go to university.

"I've still got the table you bought."

His reaction stuns her. "Don't talk like this to me, Aly!"

She's not ready for it. Her heart starts pounding before she's taken in the words.

"I'm not interested in swapping reminiscences. If that was all you wanted, you shouldn't have come."

"I didn't expect to see you," she says. It's not a lie. She didn't expect, not today, for all she hoped, and for all she would have come back again till she did.

He suddenly grins. "What were the odds?"

This sounds more like him, despite the unfamiliar edge to it.

He pushes his chair away from the table, stands up, and without a thought she gets up, too, and walks out with him, down the dark, musty hall and up the stairs.

He holds a door open for her. It's at the back of the house, and the window's open, its pleated paper blind raised. There's no musty smell here. The window overlooks a scraggly yard and beyond that a lane. In the yard is a heap of metal, welded haphazardly together.

"Someone's a sculptor?"

"Rotten, isn't it?" He's looking through a pile of CDs, and puts one on. Classical, contemporary, not something he had before.

As he crosses to the window to close it and pull down the blind, she walks over and picks up the CD case and attempts to study it. Her hand shakes. John Williams, playing Takemitsu. To the Edge of Dream for Guitar and Orchestra. Toward the Sea for Alto Flute and Guitar. *Amours perdues.* Lost loves.

"What do you think?"

"It's beautiful."

"The room."

She looks around. On the floor, over what must be the landlord's mouldy carpet, he's put straw matting. Metal desk, industrial shelving. It looks as if he's been reading a novel or two, now he doesn't have to. On the walls, corkboard, drawings, black and white photos of fanlights, fences, steps—his own pictures, matted but not framed. An aluminium office lamp. So this is what it is now. The Fifties are gone. A single bed, a navy sheet that's roughly pulled up so it doesn't quite cover the ancient striped mattress below.

"I'm pretty neat these days," he says.

"In self-defense?"

"I suppose so. And the aesthetic requires it."

She smiles, but that goes.

He comes to where she is and begins unbuttoning her blouse. Without kissing me, she thinks. How can it be? And then he does. Thank God, he can't help it. She feels the giving-in run through him.

Once his body was a slender straight line. He's always going to be slim, but even in the time they've been apart, his chest has filled out, his thighs. When she sees him naked again, it makes no difference that she regrets the boy, so violently is she aroused by the man. It's Tom.

He has scars from the accident, one just inside the hairline, from temple to ear; a web of them on his knee. She would like to kiss these scars, tenderly, but something stops her. She has no right.

He does look older. Eighteen's still only eighteen, it's not that he's acquired wrinkles, so what is it? The skin's firmer over the bones, it's lost some of that fineness under which the colour used so visibly to come and go, but that's not all. Mostly it's an expression. Nameless.

He's obviously been thinking how she's changed, too. She does in fact have a few wrinkles that weren't there before, but he doesn't mention them. "You're thinner," he says, running a hand up from belly to breast and down again. This lightest touch. Neither of them says what he used to say at first, but it happens anyhow. One more.

Once he told her he'd been reading an ancient copy of the *Kama Sutra* that his parents had around. Not so ancient; she could have told him when it dated from. But I like the simple ones best, don't you, Aly? Tom, the minimalist. Yes, I do, she said, thinking then of Eric, heavy, insistent, resentful: I know what you want He never did, and there was never any way he'd find out. Tom has never not known, or wanted to know. Not even now, when the delight that used to lead him, when later they lay quiet, to trace her brow with a forefinger, to draw a strand of her hair across his lips, to smile at her about nothing, all those little things, is apparently gone.

She used to know what it was to feel disgust, and not only that but self-disgust, after sex. She's never before felt as sad as she does now. With Tom. Is this something you can fight, too?

Seeing his instruments leaning in their cases against the wall, she asks him, "Do you have much time to play?"

"I don't play. I don't feel like it."

"I thought you'd always have it, Tom!"

"I don't feel musical any more."

She's looking at him in horror.

I would've played for you, he once said. And that was the first I knew.

He's turned his face to the grubby wall. "Why did you do it, Aly?"

Because I thought—what was it I thought? I have no answer.

"I tried as hard as I could to make you feel it was safe. To love me. You let me think it was working. I never once thought I might be making a mistake. I thought we were part of each other! I trusted you, and you gave me up. Do you know what you did?"

He's stopped himself from saying, what you did to me. He's still very young, after all, and he doesn't yet know how to keep it out of his voice.

She's too slow. He's regretted the question immediately, and he's out of bed, out of the end of it so as not to touch her again, and pulling up his jeans. His back to her.

Getting into her own clothes, at this she's quick. She wants only to get out.

On the stairs, they meet a boy who looks at her with open curiosity. The sculptor, perhaps. He'll be getting a reputation for older women, she thinks, something like that. She remembers when she was a student, the people around whom there were rumours of other than student romance, and the ones who tried to create rumours, legends even, for themselves. You probably have to do a lot more, now, to get a reputation worth having.

She gets in the car. She never even locked it, amazing it's still here. Silently he watches her drive away. That's when it comes to her, what looks familiar. It's the *Young Man Against a Background of Flames*. Once before it was the shirt, when he wore a white school shirt. Now it's the beard. His just happens to grow that way.

Stopped at a red light, she looks down. Her blouse is done up on the wrong buttons. There's the soreness and stickiness between her legs. Drive carefully. This was just something that had to be done. He for his own reasons, she for hers. It was never an opportunity.

It's losing him all over again.

A month or so later, she's kneeling, transferring vinyl pots of seedlings to a display stand, when she realises that a customer has come to stand beside her.

"So this is where you're working!" Mel's as healthy-looking as ever, all in shades of khaki: pants, shirt, hair, unglossy tan. "I'm looking for something big and green for the sunroom."

"You've finished it?"

"Looks good, too. We went with the pine panelling." Mel squats easily down beside her. "Got a minute? I've been thinking about ringing you. There's a few things I wanted to say, so I might as well say them now. I know I wasn't very understanding, Alyson. About all that."

"Please— don't worry about it, Mel."

"No. You have to realise. I'm a very conservative woman. I'm about as suburban as my mother is. I'm only really different from her in this one way, you know. Though she doesn't see it. And then there's the Superteacher thing." She pulls a face. "Bill's such a prick, but he's got a point. It's dangerous to be good at telling people what to do. It can make you arrogant."

"I never thought you were arrogant."

"Well. How about coming over? Bring him."

"We're not together any more."

A click of the tongue. "Ah. I've put my foot in it."

"No, it's a while now."

"Then come, we can talk."

What about, if not school? I can't tell a birdie from a bully-off, and I'm not renovating anything. Still, it's more than I could have expected. It's kind.

Tania calls. "Alyson, phone."

She hurries into the back room. The phone's surrounded by junk: a mug of cold tea, a trial pack of African violet food, a ball of string, a stack of angular bonsai pots, scattered plastic labels. No-one calls her at work. What could be wrong? Mum? She reaches for the receiver over a pile of spiked invoices.

She hasn't thought to hear his voice again.

"I've been trying all the plant shops in the phone book," he says. "Aly, Maura died last night."

"Oh, Tom." So much alike.

"A brain tumour. It was horrible. But fast." He's having difficulty going on, but determinedly, not giving her a chance to speak, he does. "They found it just after. Just after I saw you. The funeral's tomorrow. Will you come?"

"To the church?"

"The whole thing. It's a cremation, there's a chapel. I mean with me."

"But Tom, Louise's mother—"

"And my grandmother. And they weren't speaking, because of me. She wasn't against—" He stops short. "You knew that, you called her, Aly."

"Yes. But what about Louise?"

"She's been in Melbourne at a conference, coming back today. I'm not asking her. I just want you to come. Do this one thing for me."

Dazed, she stands by the phone till Tania puts her head around the door. "The lady wants those *Howea* palms you put out the back for her, Alyson."

She has a passably elegant grey suit, and a grey straw hat. The former was bought for the visit to the school of the Minister for Education, the latter long ago for her father's funeral. A white silk blouse, which she irons meticulously.

He doesn't come right in. He stands just inside the door. This is the first time she's ever seen him in a suit and tie. The shirt is pale grey. The beard is gone, perhaps only this morning, so clean-shaven does he appear. She doesn't comment on this, and he doesn't say, everything looks different.

She's holding her hat. He waits there while she puts it on, using her reflection in the glass of her rose print. She can't really see her face in it, she doesn't want to. She's pinned her hair up, and he says, "There's a bit at the back," and, taking a step closer, matter-of-factly he tucks it up under her hat. She has to fiddle for another moment or two, waiting for the message sent by his fingers to the base of her spine to subside.

Walking down the path to his old car, both of them grey and formal, herself in high heels for the first time in quite a while, she thinks, we must look more or less like a couple. A strange date. If that's what it is. He opens the car door for her. And he gets to drive.

At the crematorium, Louise, red-eyed, looks right through her. But they all sit in a row at the front. Louise, Toby. Griselda, Tom. And Alyson. She hesitates, but she feels the pressure of his hand on her arm, and she sits down. She can't imagine what people think, but it doesn't really matter. There's a moment during the service when he lets out something like a sob. Just once. She puts her hand on his. He's recovered. But he's forgotten his handkerchief. She's remembered to bring a proper one, plain white. She gives it to him.

Her own thoughts are of the night at the hospital, the same hospital where now Maura has died. Of her phone call to Maura. He'd be happy to hear from you. Why did she say that? She didn't know, but she wanted me to try. It would have been for him that she wanted it.

Maura's coffin, a sheaf of white lilies laid on it, lies between the velvet curtains that will soon close it off from view. What remains of Maura's spare, silvery beauty will slide into the flames. Come to dust.

Thank you, Maura, for that impulse.

On the way out, Louise falters. Closer than Toby at that moment, Tom takes her arm. Alyson drops back. People are standing in sociable clumps around the chapel door. Tom goes to get the car, Toby his. Louise is surrounded.

Katie slips through the crowd. "God, I didn't think I'd see you here, Alyson. With Tom! You're not going to the house!"

"I'm going wherever Tom wants me to go."

Katie opens her eyes wide in a pantomime of speechlessness. Tom stands by the car. "Alyson. Katie? Come with us."

"You take Griselda," says Toby.

"Wouldn't miss it for anything," says Katie, only for Alyson to hear, climbing in the back with Griselda.

He says to her as they go in, "It'll be all right." Perhaps it will. Perhaps she will be allowed to have a drink and leave with Tom and never be seen again.

Mr. and Mrs. Ng are here, in black, passing things round. She takes an almond wafer, and it's dry in her mouth. A crumb sticks in her chest. Tom hands her a sherry, and she washes it down.

This is the first time I've been in this house since the party where Tom didn't appear. Just before he was sixteen.

Where's Louise?

Oliver comes over to say, "I'm sorry, Tom. Lovely lady." He gives Tom a hug. "Long time, Alyson."

"I hear Tom's working for you," she says.

"Very able lad." Emphasis on the final word.

People seem to be watching them.

In the elderly roué manner he sometimes affects, Oliver says, "Katie, my dear, you're looking very fetching in that hat. Is it proper to say this at a funeral?"

Katie smiles under her curly brim.

"For that matter, is it proper to twinkle at a funeral?"

Tom and Alyson stand silent as Oliver leads Katie away to look down the harbour at a building of his that's still just scaffolding and cranes.

"What's it going to be like?" she finally asks.

"A monstrosity," he says.

Griselda offers a plate of cheese. King Island brie, with that faint seaweedy taste. Goes down well with another sherry.

There's Louise. People around her, some damped-down laughter.

A container ship glides by, momentarily obscuring the view of Oliver's building. A couple of yachts. A red water taxi buzzes in the foreground. Oliver calls Tom over. He wants to talk about this building. To allow youthful criticism, to be seen to deal with it generously, that's always good.

Griselda, among the crowd, looks forlorn. She's trying to be useful. "Do you miss your karate?"

"When you've got a weak spot, that's the part that always gets hurt. It's OK. It served its purpose. I'm thinking about giving rock climbing a go."

One of the many things I'm never going to do in this life, climb rocks.

There's soft music. Is there usually, at these things? "Vivaldi," says Griselda. "*Il favorito*. I put it on. It really was her favourite, they reckon she had an affair with the violinist years back. I wish I looked like her, but it's Tom that does. Makes me sick. Do you know he's not playing any more?"

"Yes."

"They blame you."

Fair enough. But all that matters is that he blames me.

"I've blamed you, too, Aly, not only for that. But it's funny, I didn't want you to throw in the towel, either. I thought you had, until Tom—" Griselda stops mid-sentence.

Louise. The knot of guests around her has parted. She looks gaunt and exhausted.

But she's starting across the room.

She will do it. This is what it will be: how dare you be here uninvited, in my home. After what you've done. At the funeral of my mother, of all people, from whom I was estranged because of you. Get out of my house!

I want very much to leave, but if I leave that way, even with Tom, it's all over. People are looking, conversations have stopped.

Tom's coming. Even if he gets here before her— No. If there's anything at all still between him and me, it won't survive any more of this. It will only remind him that I can't take it, that I failed him, and that I'll fail him again, given the opportunity. She looks terrible. I understand her passions, I've had cause to be grateful to her. Guilt and fear have been my weak spots. No point in saying any of the things I would have said, Tom wanted me to be here, Tom is still your son—Maura said that—Tom is a mourner. She's got nothing to lose. Her own mother's funeral. She has every right to be distraught. Anything goes, today. I am the intruder, the betrayer. The wrecker. Everyone here knows that.

And then another thought: if she thinks I'm still a threat, maybe I am. Maybe I still have a chance.

A dart of happiness shoots into a vein.

She steps forward to meet Louise, speaks first. "Oh, Louise! I am so sorry— Louise, are you all right? Louise? Oh!"

She clutches Louise's elbow. A Mel technique, doesn't take much actual strength, said Mel, demonstrating. Works on quite big girls, which Louise is not, rendering them immobile. Learned from Annie, who did a stint on shore patrol when she was in the Navy. I seem to be quite strong enough. It's all those bags of fertilizer. Louise's mouth is open in shock. "Are you going to be sick?" Louder voice, teacher's voice. "Try not to be sick, not yet, Louise! Tom! Griselda!"

"What's the matter?" Toby for once is confused, but can't resist taking charge when she propels Louise as hard as she dares into his arms. "Louise, sit down!" he instructs. He pushes her back into a deep beige leather armchair, shoves her head forward between her legs. "This is what you do," he says. "Blood to the brain."

Louise struggles, but Toby, bless his congealed heart, is strong, and his big hand's on the back of her neck.

"I'm all right! I'm all *right!*" she finally gasps.

"Are you sure?" asks Alyson, bending over her. To Toby she says, "Because we were just going— Tom? She's come over faint all of a sudden!"

He crouches by Louise's chair. "Shhh," he whispers, as she attempts to speak. "She knew, she knew you loved her." He thinks that's what it is.

Louise, shakily, stands. Katie is there to help. Sorry to disappoint you, Katie.

"We should go, let her rest," says Katie. Sympathetic undertones all round, glasses relinquished. Oliver downs his drink amid the manoeuvring, but as Katie makes for the door, he's right behind her. Weddings, funerals. Another self-absorbed shit for Katie.

Louise is being kissed, over and over.

When it's their turn, Louise steps back so as not to be kissed by Alyson, as if she'd rather be bitten by a funnelweb spider. Toby, though, moves forward. His lips are moist on her cheek. "Thanks for coming," he murmurs.

They're leaving, they're out of the room into the wide hallway. She glances behind. Through the archway, she sees the splendid blue view laid out in the background, the remaining guests watching them leave, and Louise standing there framed, looking—not bewildered, Louise is never, even now, bewildered—as if she's just heard something new and strange and is working on making sense of it. This time Alyson looks straight back at her.

Outside, he says, "Thank you, Aly." He means only thanks for being here. He might have a sense of something averted, but he has no way of knowing the precise nature of the battle she's just won against a bereaved woman, or even that there was a battle at all. It's not his kind of fight. She's not proud of it, primitive as her tactics were; it was only the best she could do in that moment. No matter, she thinks. It's done.

Nothing has changed between us.

He's taking her home, but before they get there, he suddenly turns into a side street, which narrows to a precipitous lane. It leads down to a point opposite a dock where a rust-streaked ship

is berthed. Some houses, a patch of bush. He parks overlooking
the water. There aren't any other cars, just a few kids fishing off
a wharf.

"I have to tell you some things, Aly."

She stares straight ahead, sitting up straight in her grey suit,
stiff with apprehension. Was the battle for nothing? "Then tell
me."

"I have to tell you what I've been doing all this time."

"Apart from studying?" Her voice is steady.

He says, "Fucking."

Now she turns away, quickly, as if she's heard something like
a shot outside. But there are only the fishermen. She makes a fist
against her mouth.

He's not going to speak again until she does.

"No doubt you've been able to get quite a lot." She sits forward again, rubs her knuckles where her teeth have bitten down
on them. It's something to do, he won't know.

"You can if you put your mind to it."

This hand is actually quivering, it wants to give me away.
Quick, hide it from him.

"Why are you telling me this, Tom?"

"Isn't it what you meant?"

"What I meant?"

"You thought that if I stayed with you, sooner or later I'd want it so much, all the experience I didn't have, someone younger, all the rest of it—in spite of everything I'd done and said, you expected me to dump you. So you threw me out first. That's what it was really about, wasn't it? Not exams. Not my future. That was the least of it."

"Yes, it's what I meant," she says bleakly. Isn't that how it's supposed to be?

"It's a strange thing. You mightn't have been wrong. I don't know," he says. "But that's why I'm telling you. I've done my best. I'm aging as fast as I can."

The water is choppy and grey. The ship is loading coal. A crane moves slowly in front of a black hill. "Is this all? You just wanted to tell me this?"

"No. I want to tell you I realise that you never made me any promises. You couldn't help it if I'd always got everything I wanted, if I couldn't imagine not getting it. And I was younger then, I thought I knew everything and I thought it was simple. You knew it wasn't. You tried not to encourage me."

"Yes and no. You don't have to be quite that fair to me."

"I didn't hear all the things that were said to you. You were trying to protect me. But I knew when I was in the hospital they'd get to you, without me there, and I couldn't do a thing to stop it. I can guess how it was done. They had the advantage of you, Aly."

She remembers his temper and frustration those last weeks in the hospital.

"You know how stupid I am." She can't claim credit with him for a sacrifice he didn't want or need.

"Did I say that?"

"Yes."

"That wasn't right. If you'd been the kind of person that could deal with them on their own terms, you wouldn't have been you, and then I mightn't have loved you so much."

She's still worrying about the past tense, the conditionals, when he says, "Aly. I've been thinking. You were still shocked from the accident. You had to have been."

He's making an excuse for her that she hasn't made herself, but it is true.

"It was the worst night of my life." This too is true, though there have been very bad nights since.

And he didn't die. He's sitting here beside her, no longer an eager, confident boy, but a man in a grey suit, saying: I've been thinking.

"I should have thought of that before," he says. "How it must have been for you. But I couldn't, not until I saw you. I was too angry. That was what got me through the exams, through every-thing. I was never going to come near you again." He's looking at the ship. Her eyes are on him. "I thought you were never going to come near me. And when you did, I was still angry. I never would have thought I could stay so angry for so long. That's why it was how it was. I'm sorry, Aly. But it wasn't until after that I could start to think."

"I didn't come only the once. I came till I saw you."

He doesn't hear her. He's wrestling with something more. "Have you been going with anyone else?"

"No."

"It's been on my mind."

"It needn't have been."

"You would have eventually."

"I don't know about eventually."

It's slipping away, the opportunity.

She couldn't be more afraid if she were clinging again to the rock at the top of the waterfall, scared to go forward or back.

Let go.

"Tom, could you trust me again?"

He shows no surprise at the question. He answers it carefully, slowly. "I want to say yes."

Nothing he said to her in the past was ever equivocal, was ever not wholehearted. She feels the words as a blow, worse than the first, that she takes straight in the chest. She puts her hand to her breastbone, too late to deflect it. She thinks, unbelieving, he has hurt me. Tom has hurt me.

But he's talking to her, that's all. And it can't begin to compare with the blow she dealt him, with how that must have hurt.

Why should he trust her?

She thinks of how she left him sitting on the hospital bed, white-faced, immobilized by his cast. His unbelief. That because of her he cried. She thinks of him facing them after that, forced to listen to the things they must have said. What they must have said about her! All he'd so gladly given up to be with her gone for nothing, a boy's foolishness. And blind refusal the only defence she'd left to him: refusal to go home, refusal to play.

But I've thought it all out, he said, that day when they stood with the width of the door between them after he first kissed her, after she first kissed him. She thinks, I didn't take him seriously. How well he already knew himself. That was my mistake. Not the kiss.

It's as if neither of them is ever going to move again.

"It's not only me," he says at last. "You never had time to decide anything. It all just happened."

"Yes." That was what was so wonderful, and so hard.

"Aly, we can't think straight, here."

"Where can we go?" He doesn't mean to go to her place. Not for thinking straight.

He can still catch her off balance. "I'm going to Italy."

"Italy." Inanely, she repeats the word.

"You know I've been saving up for it."

That's what his savings were for. I didn't know. I should have.

"Maura knew she was dying. She wanted to give Griselda and me some money, a present, separate from the will. Most of that goes to charity. I told her that's how I'd use mine."

She sits up. The silence has retreated, feeling returns.

"I'm thinking about spaces," he says. "Not only buildings. What surrounds them, what they surround. That's why I'm going. And just to go. I've been crazy to get away. Now I think, if you came, we could be together, and we could see."

See.

"When are you going?"

"Saturday. It's the vacation."

"I couldn't get a ticket!"

"You can. I checked this morning."

"Before the funeral?"

"Yes. And Aly, I've got enough money for both of us."

"I've got some, too." I've got my savings.

I made this happen, she thinks. I called his grandmother, who's now dead. I found where he was, I went there. I took the risk. Just in time, I saw him. That made today possible. I've fought as I never thought I could. And now this. Now I see my opportunity.

She's still wearing her funeral hat. She takes it off, holds it on her knee. "It's a lot further than the mountains."

"That wasn't a bad idea, the mountains," he says, unsmiling. He's not interested in reminiscences, he's said that. "Not in itself."

CHAPTER ELEVEN

*S*he came out dancing.

Now there's only seeing. Waiting to see. But what is it they're waiting for? What sign that will make all things clear again, set them free from the spell that makes them so deathly courteous, keeps their limbs from touching except in response to a most specific desire, places an invisible barrier between them when their eyes happen to meet, so, learning nothing, they look away?

From the first, when they met by the check-in queue, it didn't feel right.

When they asked for seats together, they were given them an aisle apart. The plane was full now; she must have got one of the last tickets. There was no way to talk. She tried to sleep, couldn't. He listened to something on his headphones most of the way. Sometimes he'd get up to stretch his legs; she'd see him up at the back of the plane, slouching by a window, gazing out. Once she was half-asleep and he picked up the blanket that had fallen from her knees and laid it over her again, but without touching her.

So they travelled as strangers, until they arrived in the late afternoon at the cheap hotel in Rome that was on the top floors of a shabby building, where a woman behind the desk handed them their key with a muttered word, and where without eating or drinking or unpacking they lay on the bed and turned urgently towards each other, and then slept.

She opened her eyes to the shadows of pigeons flitting across the wall and over the ceiling. Very early, some noisy delivery being made outside in the street. His eyes are still more grey than blue in the morning light. She got up and found a glass in the broken-tiled bathroom, drank, brought him water, and they made love again. Or something very close, which if they didn't know what they know, they could easily have mistaken for it. They know each other this intimately, and yet hardly at all.

He understands much more of the language than she does. It's always been there for him, in his family and in his music. He sings—he used to sing in it. His keen ear is always attuned to a new phrase. Still, they both move in a haze of incomprehension of the things people say to each other in the street, the things people say to them.

That first morning, only minutes after they walked outside, a motor scooter zipped up beside her, a hand reached out and plucked her bag from her shoulder. She simply stood there watching Tom racing down the street, around the corner, out of her sight. She hardly moved until he came back, carrying her bag, triumphant. He was happy to have been able to run as fast as that, his knee passed the test, and he'd saved her money and her passport, everything. Caught up with him in a jam in a little street, he said, bending over with his hands on his thighs to get his breath back. Told him no police if he handed it over. I had him. Wasn't bad about it really.

She should have hugged him and laughed. It might have been the thing they were waiting for, at the beginning, when it would have counted. Instead, her arms and her tongue were paralysed by the aftermath of fear. How he flung himself unthinking from the train, how he swerved on a road slick with rain at the sight of the eyes of a possum. How many ways there are to lose him.

She tried to make light of it later, at the foot of the Spanish Steps, when they saw the curvy young women cops with tons of curly black hair and big submachine guns over their shoulders. You could have called one of them, she said. He gave her a level glance, and let it pass.

He hasn't been sightseeing exactly, he's looking in a particular way. It's the buildings and their details, but most of all now, as he said, it's the spaces. When they sit in the piazza he's studying lines and proportions and where sculpture is placed and where people are walking to and from, and where selling things.

There is a point at which their interests overlap. In courtyards and cloisters, she thinks of the condition of leaf and flower, he of the function of path and urn. She at least takes pleasure in understanding what it is he notices, what concerns him. Whether or not it matters to him that he understands the same of her, as he still must, she no longer knows.

She hasn't been following him when he wanders around taking photos, she won't cling to him or crowd him. She has him in sight, she's never not aware of him, but when he turns and his eyes seek her out, she thinks, what are we seeing?

Once they were passing an expensive hotel, its glass doors flanked by footed troughs of geraniums, whose effect she'd paused to admire, and he said, that place was in Maura's album, it was where she had her first honeymoon. (I was conceived in Rome, said Louise a long time ago. Toby, he swears he senses an affinity. You can laugh, Alyson, he's a fantastic man!) I told Maura, Tom said, that you came to see me. She was pretty sick by then, but I could see she was glad.

How little pleasure, she thinks now, they gave anyone other than themselves by being in love. Or received because of it. Being teased, being looked at indulgently. That's part of it, especially when you're young like Tom. What he knew, what they most provoked, was rage, consternation, embarrassment, mirth with nothing of kindness in it.

He's grateful that Maura was glad for him, too late though it might have been.

From Florence he sent a postcard, an ordinary postcard of the Piazza della Signoria. She saw it lying on the bed: *Aly is here with me.*

She hasn't written to her own mother. She wouldn't know what to say.

In Rome and Florence, they were not noticed, or if they were, it was as an example of a phenomenon so common among tourists for so long as to be not worth remarking.

Here in Siena, at the pensione, it is remarked. There's a trio of American women not much older than herself, but thinner and with more skilfully coloured hair, whose glances say quite clearly how they read the situation. Though why, if that were so, they'd be staying in a place like this, with its good simple food, its sitting room with glass bookcase full of pre-war English walking tour guides, and ancient creaking elevator, rather than in the kind of place you'd take a youth to if you planned to drape him in silk designer shirts and gold chains, she can't imagine. And if he were her gigolo, surely they'd be all over each other, instead of as they are, always a little apart, and this serious.

But the beard, briefly there in Rome, is gone again; his hair has grown longer and fairer, he's brought sneakers and not the boots, he's only eighteen, and still as graceful. She wishes she could enjoy it, the way they look at him.

The front of the pensione looks over a narrow street, with a church and a tobacconist; the back, from their room, over the city wall and into the countryside, where in the mornings smoke rises from piles of pruned olive branches and long shadows of cypress trees fall over a narrow valley.

She spends a lot of time just leaning on the window-sill, looking out. He has his sketchbook, and he's sketched her there in the foreground, but she's indistinct, a few lines only, and her face is always turned away. When she looked over his shoulder, he said, you know I never could do figures.

He might take a photo of something, and she might be somewhere in the picture, but it is not of her.

Today they had a picnic sitting on a wall in the shade. Bread and ham, a wedge of panforte and a handful of ricciarelli cookies, an apple and a pear, a bottle of mineral water and a half of

Chianti. She gave him most of her bread, and he ate it, and both the apples, then sat with his hands clasped loosely around his knees staring at nothing. For her, every moment is a crumb of memory. But then, when you collect a memory the moment is dead.

This isn't how he meant it to be, how either of them hoped it would be. Things change, you have to expect that, but what they have now is completely out of joint with what was. They're out in the world, with nothing to say.

There's a music school here, and walking under its windows this morning they heard a violin lesson. The repeated phrase, a murmur of voices, then the music pouring out. Neither of them said anything, Tom only briefly looking up as if making a mental note of some detail of the period. He knows how to protect himself, distance himself. It was never what he wanted to know. The terrible thing is, it is from her that he learned the necessity.

In this she was his teacher.

The Piazza del Campo is the most perfectly proportioned public space imaginable, he says. Scallop-shaped or fan-shaped, whichever you call it; slightly, precisely tilted. Eleven narrow streets run into it. Through the day, the light moves across the facades of the buildings around it, and until late at night, these summer nights, people walk over its stones, for the pleasure of it.

Families and lovers. Sedate lovers, for the most part, under the eyes of those same families, their own.

So Alyson and Tom have walked, alone, across the wide piazza, then up through the quiet lanes.

The dark is warm. The stones underfoot hold the warmth from the day's sun, and from the suns of other days.

There's an unhurried movement in a stone-wreathed doorway, a hand on an iron ring. Light catches on a patch of broken plaster, the edge of a green shutter. It illuminates for a moment a relief of the Virgin and Child set in a niche, a knot of wax flowers. A door thuds softly closed, and it's darker than before.

A narrow arch, and then this quiet space. Above, the white pinnacles of the Duomo, and all their saints and angels, floodlit and moonlit.

The new cathedral was a building never built, abandoned because of the plague. It's not a ruin but an idea sketched out in stone, he says. Here, where its walls meet those of other centuries, they hear singing.

The piazza has deep corners. From one of these, close by, first comes murmuring, laughter, the waver of a flashlight. Then the notes of a guitar, and a voice. A girl's voice, not girlish. There are five or six boys and girls, sitting on some steps beneath a colonnade. A boy plays the guitar, another boy holds the music.

The song that floats out of the shadows has all of youth in it.

Tom, half-smiling, never takes his eyes off the girl while she sings. The only light is on the music, and it reflects dimly upwards onto the young face.

The song is finished, and there's whispering, conferring, riffling of pages.

He looks down at her and his expression is intent.

There's no doubt what this is about.

He's waiting.

She says, "You expected too much of me, Tom. I've tried to make it up to you."

"Is that what you've been doing?"

"So you'd trust me again."

"If you think that's all I wanted, you haven't understood anything."

"What do you want?"

"If you don't know now."

Too late.

He says, "I wanted you to trust me."

This could be a bad night, for all that they're together.

It's decided, what to play next, what to sing.

From his sudden stillness, Tom knows.

A few notes after, she knows, too.

Amarilli mia bella . . . Don't you believe, my heart's delight, that you're the one I love.

The first time she heard it, he was only just learning it, and she stood in the kitchen with the knife in her hand, overcome. Not by words she recognised, though barely understood, as conventional words of love. By Tom's voice. By having Tom.

Take my arrow, open up my breast, and you'll see engraved on my heart: *Amarilli e 'l mio amore.* Amaryllis is my love. If he stumbled and had to begin again, that only made it worse for her. She'd have done anything not to let him see.

To hear his song now robs her of all thought.

Until, as they stand there together in the dark, the girl's voice wrapping them round with a fullness drawn out of the spaces between stones, it comes to her: it isn't so strange. Not when it's Tom who's brought me to this place, and when this music is a part of him.

A woman and a boy catch sight of each other one afternoon on a train, an old man trips, a possum darts across a wet road. These are the things you can never foretell, the true coincidences.

Out of all the things that happen, on all the journeys you make, in only a few will you ever see a meaning. You take them if you can or if you must, and let the rest go. The ones you keep, they're yours.

He says, "It was always for you, Aly. I can't ever take it back."
One last chance.

She's incapable of saying his name. She draws a shaky breath, does what she did that first day. She takes his face in her hands. And it's like it was.

The voice, diminishing, follows them across the square.
They're looking for the darkest corner.

He pulls her into it, stands over her the way he never did when they fought, presses her with the length of his body hard against the wall. Tom's body is warm, the old stone still has in it the warmth of the afternoon. "I'm eighteen," he says. If he didn't come straight to the point, he wouldn't be Tom. "Aly, no-one can stop us now! We can get married."

This is enough, she thinks. It is, for me. But I've been wrong before. And there is a world.

"Listen, Aly," he says urgently. "I mean this. If you mean it too, let's just do it. So everybody knows we mean it. I don't want any more fucking around."

He can still do it, make her laugh and cry at once. "I don't think that's the way you're supposed to say it, Tom!"

"It's not the kind of thing you can get any practise at," he says, reasonably enough. "This is it." He draws away only so as to see her face, turns it towards what there is of light. "There's no need to cry, Aly. Not now. We've lasted this long. We never gave up thinking about each other. And see, we've come back to each other," he says. What she hears in his voice now is a pride that touches her to a point fleetingly indistinguishable from pain.

Three years it's been, counting from that first kiss. A long time for him, not less somehow for me. And still not sweet and twenty, Tom. Not half my age yet.

"You are sure, aren't you, Aly? You haven't ever been sorry we began?"

"You asked me something like this once before."

"A lot of things have happened since then."

"I have never been sorry," she answers soberly.

He opens his mouth to speak, but he stops, looks away.

Don't you cry, Tom. I couldn't bear it. And I'll never ask you this question, because one thing you haven't learned is how to lie to me.

But he thinks he owes her an answer, and he says, with difficulty, "When I was angry, Aly. It doesn't count."

She touches his cheek, gently.

Then he says, "Maybe it does. But it doesn't change anything. I've always known what I wanted. Haven't I shown you? I never would have got over you. I don't get over things very easily. I'm faithful." She senses his flush in the darkness. "I mean, I will be if you let me."

"I know."

He lets out a long, quiet breath.

Instinctively, she shifts against him, the old wall at her back. An almost imperceptible, nonetheless elemental movement. Before words or even thought. And Tom has understood it. As simple as that.

With his accustomed competence, and something new—a sort of possessiveness, she thinks, offering up her face, that he's surely earned—he smooths her hair back from her forehead, wipes her eyes with his fingers. And it's as if just now they can't tell which of them is the older and which the younger.

"We might even be really ordinary," he tells her, "except for this one thing."

He's never been afraid of this one thing. Both passion and constancy are in his nature, he knows that, and their source. He's seen desire frittered away, steadfastness harden into implacability. He believes he's found a harmony between them, his deepest need, in loving her. Beside this, nothing matters. Not his age or hers, not what anyone else has thought or said. Not even, in the end, her own betrayal.

She's proud too, that she's done what she had to do to make it right, but that she ever turned him away, ever brought herself to cause him hurt for no other reason than that he was young, seems incredible to her now.

"Aly?" Her silence has brought a note of uncertainty to his voice.

"I'm sure, Tom."

His smile of pure happiness is like the sun.

Later, with a sudden return of something like fear, she asks him, "What if we hadn't heard the song?" What if the music hadn't caught us, given us something to hold on to when we were about to fall beyond each other's reach?

He's full of confidence again. "There would have had to be something, Aly. When we'd come so far."

She takes his hand from her breast, separately and tenderly kisses each slender, responsive finger. "Tom, will you play again?"

"How could I not want to play, as long as I can make you cry?" he says.

In the plane going home, they'll be in luck, they'll get three seats all to themselves, and they'll sleep curled up, off and on. The sound of the window shades being slotted back will wake them, the light will flood in over yawning people, heaps of blankets, shoes, newspapers. There'll be silent golfers flickering on the video screen. A smell of bacon. Women expecting to be met will disappear into the restrooms with cosmetic bags ahead of the queue and not come out. Babies whose ears are hurting will begin to wail. He'll lean behind her in her window seat as they begin the descent. There'll be the glitter of the harbour, turquoise swimming pools, boats, bridges, Opera House, Oliver's monstrosity, gas tanks. A windy, clear morning. "Over there," he'll say, and they'll try to make out the point, the park, his parents' house.

Then the creaking and whining, the bump, the whistling down the runway.

They'll open up the flat. He'll dump the bags in the middle of the floor, look around the living room, and tell her the first thing they've got to do, absolutely, is get that coffee table out of here, and the second is radically rethink the florals.

"We'll keep the bed," he'll say. "You won't let me get a grey metal industrial-strength one, will you, Aly?"

He'll fall with his arms around her, in joyous relief, into the bed where she first brought him. Properly, he said, knowing how it should be.

Then, like a thorn when carelessly you grasp the stem of a rose, a memory will prick her brain, causing her to draw as sharp a breath. That morning when her hand, repeatedly, in mounting panic, swept the sheet searching for him and found him gone. The mornings that followed. Do what you want with the bed, Tom!

But he won't be thinking of it any more.

∞

Afterwards, he'll throw back his head and shake the hair out of his eyes, and say, "Breakfast." And she'll kiss his throat, sheened with sweat, and laugh at him, refuse to let him go from her. She will have forgotten, too.

It will be too bright to sleep, anyhow.

On the balcony, her hastily rigged watering system will have broken down and the wind will have blown dried-out leaves around.

He'll undo string and cardboard and scatter straw all over the place to make sure the cheap ceramic plates they managed to agree on have survived the trip. One's chipped. "Don't worry, Aly, I'll mend it so you won't know," he'll promise.

She'll look at it in his hands and think: we've got things. Tom and I.

This is him. This is me.

Toby will be standing at the door, with a bottle of champagne. For later. "Had an idea I might find you here," he'll say. "Well. You made it. Home." Fumbling, unlike Toby, for the tone he needs. "When are you going to make up your mind about the beard, mate?"

Tom will be in the kitchen seeing if there's beer, and Toby

will ask her, curious, "What does your mother think about all this?"

"She loves him."

"When did she meet him?"

"She hasn't yet."

Then he'll say, "You should have got tough sooner, Aly. There was never any doubt in my mind that you could win. I have to know when I've lost, and I wouldn't have risked any more."

If she starts to speak, she'll say, you fool, what did you think you were doing?

"Louise, on the other hand—" He'll look for a way to say it. "Louise doesn't know the first thing about losing."

Louise will come by to pick Toby up, but she won't come in, so Tom will go downstairs to see her. Alyson will go out on the balcony to water her plants. They need it badly.

A flutter of brilliant wings, and a lorikeet will appear on the parapet, then another. She'll say to them, playfully, don't go away, but an unexpected surge of emotion will tear at the words. He's here, she'll mean to say.

Louise's car will be parked just below, and he'll be leaning against it, long legs crossed at the ankle, arms folded, completely at ease. At something he says, Louise, beside him, will look up sharply, her hair blowing over her face.

Alyson won't pretend not to see, standing on the windy balcony with her watering can in her hands. She'll be feeling a bit dizzy, that lasting strangeness you have after a long overnight flight, the hollow feeling in the head from noise and sleeplessness, and now this quiet, the fresh salty wind.

Louise will put on her dark glasses, get in the car. He'll tap on her window, she'll roll it down, he'll say one last thing. He will never not offer her something. He'll step back, and as Louise drives away he'll turn and walk out of Alyson's line of vision.

She'll hear him say good morning to someone on the stairs. She'll leave her plants, wiping her hands on her shirt, go to meet him.

He'll come in the open door, and on the wall behind him there'll be a dazzling patch of morning sun. As the wind shifts in the trees outside, it will flicker and leap, like flames.

She won't be able to make out his face at first, but when she does, it will be the face of the boy on the train, lit up at the sight of her.

"We're on our own, Aly," he'll say.